Praise for Jonathan Galassi's

Muse

"A testament to the purity of the written word and the turmoil that can be required to get it on paper."

—*The New Yorker*

"Keenly observed. . . . Incisive. . . . *Muse*—much like John Updike's early Bech books—leaves insiders with a knowing portrait of the publishing world before the digital revolution, and gives outsiders an entertaining, gently satirical look at the passions and follies of a vocation peopled by 'fanatics of the cult of the printed word.'"

—*The New York Times*

"Make[s] poetry and publishing feel alive with complexity and drama and feeling. . . . How beautifully Galassi represents moments of literary triumph." —*Commonweal*

"Charming. . . . It is one of the pleasures of *Muse* to watch Galassi mix his fictional literati with the real ones."

—*The New York Review of Books*

"A long-awaited, and worthwhile, event. Galassi's main character is the heir to a prestigious publishing house who becomes the confidante of his favorite writer, a poet whose personal life is as famed as her writing."

—*Vanity Fair*

"Packed with lively secrets and insider gossip from the world of literature." —*Entertainment Weekly*

"Beguiling. . . . Galassi imbues his offbeat tale with emotional intensity and a lingering resonance."
—*Miami Herald*

"An enjoyably incestuous tangle of life and art. . . . Preserve[s] the quirks and charms of a colorful era in literary culture." —*The Boston Globe*

"Accomplished. . . . Affecting. . . . *Muse* adds still another gold star to Jonathan Galassi's literary report card."
—*New York Journal of Books*

"A fictional send-up of New York's publishing industry, by one of its real-life members. . . . While industry insiders will likely recognize the thinly veiled references to key players in publishing, outsiders will giggle at Galassi's accounts of aggressive agents, arrogant authors and barbaric book fairs." —*New York Post*

"A witty, elegant, tons-of-fun debut novel. Jonathan Galassi has got all the dirt on the publishing industry and he is ready to *dish*. But he also takes us from Union Square and a hideaway country cottage to Venice, for a love story all his own." —Gary Shteyngart

Jonathan Galassi

Muse

Jonathan Galassi is the president and publisher of Farrar, Straus & Giroux and the author of three collections of poetry, as well as acclaimed translations of the Italian poets Eugenio Montale and Giacomo Leopardi. A former Guggenheim Fellow and poetry editor of *The Paris Review*, he also writes for *The New York Review of Books* and other publications.

Also by Jonathan Galassi

POETRY

Left-handed

North Street

Morning Run

TRANSLATIONS

Annalisa Cima, *Hypotheses on Love*

Giacomo Leopardi, *Canti*

Eugenio Montale, *Collected Poems, 1920–1954*

Eugenio Montale, *Otherwise: Last and First Poems*

Eugenio Montale, *Posthumous Diary*

Eugenio Montale, *The Second Life of Art: Selected Essays*

Muse

Muse

A Novel

Jonathan Galassi

VINTAGE BOOKS
A Division of Penguin Random House LLC
New York

FIRST VINTAGE BOOKS EDITION, JUNE 2016

The Library of Congress has cataloged the Alfred A. Knopf edition as follows:
Galassi, Jonathan.
Muse : a novel / Jonathan Galassi.
pages ; cm
I. Title.
PS3557.A387M87 2015 813'.54—dc23 2014025424

Vintage Books Trade Paperback ISBN: 978-0-8041-7249-3
eBook ISBN: 978-0-385-35335-9

Book design by M. Kristen Bearse

www.vintagebooks.com

Printed in the United States of America
10 9 8 7 6 5 4 3 2 1

For my heroes
(you know who you are);

for Beatrice and Isabel,
my heroines;

and in loving memory of Ida Perkins

Muse

This is a love story. It's about the good old days, when men were men and women were women and books were books, with glued or even sewn bindings, cloth or paper covers, with beautiful or not-so-beautiful jackets and a musty, dusty, wonderful smell; when books furnished many a room, and their contents, the magic words, their poetry and prose, were liquor, perfume, sex, and glory to their devotees. These loyal readers were never many but they were always engaged, always audible and visible, alive to the romance of reading. Perhaps they still exist underground somewhere, hidden fanatics of the cult of the printed word.

For these happy few, literature was life, and the slowly burning pages on which it took shape were the medium of their cult. Books were revered, cherished, hoarded, collected, given, and sometimes borrowed, though seldom returned. The rarity of an item—the number of copies in an edition, the beauty and complexity of its printing, occasionally the quality of its contents—determined its value. Once in a great while, a book was deemed to be worth millions. Works that bore the signature of their authors were objects of veneration, displayed under lock and key in the inner sancta of great libraries and museums. Writers—in those days, only a few assumed the mantle of authorship, a demanding and even dangerous vocation—were the high priests of this religion, shunned and held in suspicion by the unwashed but idolized by the initiated faithful.

This is the story of some of the truest of this religion's true believers. They came into their own in the heady days after World War II when everything seemed possible, and in subtle ways they changed the culture they lived in, made it richer, deeper, more exciting and full of promise. Richness and depth are qualities not much in vogue in these days of speed and instantaneous transformation. Our virtual world is a flat world, and we relish this about it. We change identities at the drop of a hat; we pivot, regroup, reconfigure, reinvent. The characters in this story are different. They were loyal to their own sometimes twisted yet settled natures, modern in the old-fashioned sense. And in their own selfish ways, they were heroes.

This is also the story of our country's love affair with one of its great poets. Ida Perkins streaked across the sky of American life and letters as a very young woman and remained there in one way or another until her death in 2010 at the age of eighty-five. While she lived, her every word and movement was noted and commented on, lionized, bemoaned. Our critics—most of them, anyway—fell down before her, but so did the commonest of common readers. She made poetry fans out of ordinary women and men, and when she died, the outpouring of national grief was such that President Obama designated her death day, which was also her birthday, a national holiday.

All of Ida's many lovers remained devoted to her; and all of them searched for, and found, reflections of themselves and of her love for each of them in her poems. But there were others who pined for her in unrequited fashion, who could know her only through her words—the readers who faithfully bought book after book over Ida's long career; the editors who dreamed of publishing her; the young poets who sat at her feet when she let them and swooned to be her swains; the critics who continue today to discover and invent the meanings of her infinitely various oeuvre; and the scholars who for decades to come will be poring over the many writings she left behind: poems, essays, unfinished memoirs and fiction and plays, and notebooks, many of them as yet unavailable—everything but letters, for Ida never wrote, or kept, personal correspondence. Presumably she received countless missives from admirers as various as Pound, Eliot, Avery, Moore, Stevens, Montale, Morante, Winslow, Char, Adams, Lowell, Plath, Olson, Kerouac, Ginsberg, Cheever, Hummock, Burack, Erskine, O'Hara, Merrill, Gunn, Snell, Vezey, Styron, Ashbery, Popa, Bachmann, Milosz, Merwin, Sontag, Carson, Nielsen, Glück, Cole, and McLane—to name only a few of her closest literary associations. But though she no doubt read many of their letters, as far as we can tell she kept none of them, and all of her correspondents knew better than to expect a reply. Words, for

Ida, were meant to be whispered conspiratorially (and deniably), or else committed irrevocably to the page. Her instantly recognizable breathy voice—for a high-wattage intellectual star, she came across as exceedingly shy—was part and parcel of what her second and by common consensus most beloved husband, Stephen Roentgen, called her "lifelong need to seem normal."

Ida disliked talking about literature; she felt it was dull, unworthy: shoptalk. Cooking, gardening, pictures, sex, and politics were her preferred topics of conversation. And gossip. Always gossip. She was reputedly one of the world's best storytellers, though with a forgiving lilt to her voice that could make the worst crimes come across as mere peccadilloes.

Among her most loyal acolytes were two of the significant publishers of her time: Sterling Wainwright, founder and presiding genius of prestigious, influential Impetus Editions, who was also her second cousin, first love, and principal publisher; and Homer Stern, king of Purcell & Stern, Sterling's brash and brassy rival, who long carried a torch for Ida—and may have extinguished it at least once or twice in Ida's early New York years. And there was Paul Dukach, who had the luck to be a young editor at the right moment at Homer's scrappy but consequential firm. Paul worshipped Ida from afar, with a devotion that sometimes made him sick with yearning unworthiness—the kind of feverish attachment that if you're not careful can burn its unknowing object to a crisp. Eventually, this young man's passion for Ida would transform the trajectory of her work and change the lives of all of them.

We make so much of love. We live for it, we ache for it, we convince ourselves that we'll die without it and make the search for it the focus of our lives. Yet love, my friends, is a terrible pain. It distracts us; it sucks up time and energy, makes us listless and miserable when we're without it and turns us into bovine creatures when we find it. Being in love is arguably the least productive of human states. It is not, as so many believe, synonymous with happiness. So when I say this is a love story, I'm telling you it's not entirely a happy story. It is what it is—the raw truth, the fabric of our heroes' and heroine's messy lives, the scent of their days and nights, the marrow of their souls. Proceed with caution.

I

Homer and Company

"Fuck the peasants!"

That ancient cry off the Russian steppe was the trademark toast of Homer Stern, founder, president, and publisher of the tony, impecunious independent publishing house Purcell & Stern. He raised a glass with it often at dinners celebrating his authors' victories or, better yet, defeats, after the numerous award ceremonies that punctuate the publishing year. Homer's salute to his warriors divided the world cleanly into *us* and *them*—or maybe it was *me* and *them*—a spot-on reflection of his Hun-like worldview.

Homer was a womanizer, and he made no particular effort to hide it. It was part of the broad advertisement of self that some found disarming and just as many detested. To his fellows, his frank appreciation of female horseflesh jibed with his loud, nasal upper-class New York accent and loud, expensive clothes—"On him they look good," Carrie Donovan allowed in the pages of *Harper's Bazaar*—and his taste for Cuban cigars and Mercedes convertibles. It had taken him years to buy a German car after the war, but his fondness for luxury and display eventually won out over any lingering historical or religious compunctions. Homer exuded a kind of leftover, gently down-at-the-heels German Jewish droit du seigneur that was only slightly put on. He'd inherited it from his father, the grandson of a lumber baron who'd made a fortune out West when the First Transcontinental Railroad needed ties by the boxcar. That was a long time ago, though, and the Stern family coffers were nowhere near as full of dollars as they had been, after three generations of dilution without replenishment. As with many who live on inherited wealth, Homer's sense of what money can buy hadn't kept pace with inflation. He was a famously chintzy tipper.

Still, he reveled in the *bella figura* that let him give the impression of being much better off than he was. He once told his son Plato that looking rich made it easier to put off paying his printing bills; his printer of choice, Sonny Lenzner, would always assume he could pay up when he got around to it. As his wife, Iphigene Abrams, likewise an heiress, to a faded Newark department store fortune, was quoted as saying, not without pride (they had married almost in arranged fashion at twenty-one and were to remain together through thick and thin for sixty-three years), "Homer likes nothing better than walking a tightrope over the abyss." Iphigene published a series of neo-Proustian memoir-novels in the seventies and eighties that had been highly regarded by some. Many were amused by her Edwardian-era bluestocking affectations—billowing chiffon gowns and garden hats, or jodhpurs and riding crop—as if she wanted it to be known she was a throwback and proud of it. She was the perfect foil to Homer's Our Crowd Mafioso showiness. They made quite a pair.

Stern was the last of the independent "gentlemen" publishers, scions of Industrial Revolution fortunes of greater or lesser magnitude who'd decided to spend what remained of their inheritance on something that was fun for them and perhaps generally worthwhile, too. College right after the war—he'd attended a series of institutions of descending degrees of seriousness, always managing to get himself thrown out before graduation—was followed by a stint in the army's public relations branch, where he'd done his damnedest to sell enlistment via jingle and poster to a conflict-weary public. He'd also acquired a penchant for inventive profanity, which, combined with the Yiddishisms he'd picked up later on, when he and Iphigene got interested in their Jewish roots, made for a delicious idiomatic goulash all his own.

When Homer set out, in the dark days of the fifties, to start a publishing house with Heyden Vanderpoel, a wealthy WASP tennis buddy of his, he'd invited Frank Purcell—"Like the composer," he invariably said on being introduced, in case someone might mistakenly put the accent on the second syllable—to join them. Frank was a once-celebrated editor from an older generation who'd been unceremoniously cut loose from his previous job while he was off in Korea. In the end, Vanderpoel's mother had objected to his linking his impeccable name with a Jew's, and Heyden hadn't wanted to work nine to five anyway, so it was just Homer and Frank: Stern and Purcell. Or Purcell and Stern, as Frank had insisted, reasonably enough. They set up shop and waited for something to happen.

Eventually something had. The fledgling company struggled along for a while on the occasional commercial best seller: nutrition bibles and the collected speeches of various governors and secretaries of state—remember, this was the fifties—with now and then a high-toned foreign novel recommended by one or another of Homer's European scouts, pals from his army days now working, some muttered sotto voce, as undercover operatives for the CIA. It wasn't until the mid-sixties, though, that Homer convinced Georges Savoy, a French émigré with a genuine feeling for writing and a well-stocked stable acquired during a productive but turbulent career at Owl House, to come work with him and Frank that Purcell & Stern jelled. Soon enough, through the alchemical fusion of Georges's taste and connections with Homer's salesmanship—not to mention the contributions of a series of young staffers who slaved twelve or fourteen hours a day at abysmal wages for the privilege of being associated with Greatness—P & S emerged as a force to contend with in literary publishing, a kind of rocket of originality.

It wasn't just Pepita Erskine, the taboo-smashing firebrand African American critic and novelist, who set the tone at the firm. There was Iain Spofford, the pernickety New Journalist who ruled at *The Gothamite*, known to many as "*The Newer Yorker*," which had recently emerged as America's premier cultural weekly. There were Elspeth Adams, queen of the icy sonnet, and Winthrop Winslow, the confessional Brahmin novelist, and the scholarly, subtly subversive critic Giovanni Di Lorenzo—writers who were defining a generation in letters and who introduced Homer and Georges to a gifted younger generation, among them the trio of eventual Nobel Prize–winning poets whom Homer dubbed the Three Aces.

And there was Thor Foxx. Thornton Jefferson Foxx was a not-so-good ol' boy from the hills of Tennessee with a Colonel Sanders goatee who swore like a trucker and whose irreverent debunking of New York literary pretension had won him instant fame in the pretension-strewn canyons of Gotham. Thor and Pepita were the proverbial oil and water, and it was a tribute to Homer and Iphigene's Fred and Ginger–like social skills that these two cornerstones of the P & S list could show up simultaneously in the crush of one of the Sterns' coveted at-homes in their stylishly moderne East Eighty-third Street town house and not bump into each other.

So P & S surprisingly quickly became a legend in publishing circles. And that was where the trouble between Homer and Sterling Wainwright began. P & S came to be regarded as the smallest, scrappiest, and most "literary" of the "major" publishers, while Wainwright's Impetus Editions, for all its cultural impact and influence (Sterling had had half a decade's head start on Homer, to be fair), was considered the largest and most esteemed of the small presses, another world altogether. And though Homer was stingy with author advances, Impetus was cheaper still—much, much cheaper. Even so, there was significant overlap, and when the cocky young Jewish American writer Byron Hummock left Impetus for P & S after the publication of his prizewinning book of stories, *All Around Sheboygan*, war was declared. And it had never ended.

Wainwright, a card-carrying WASP from Ohio whose inheritance (ball bearings) trumped Stern's by a factor of ten (some said much more), regarded Homer as a crass and ill-mannered upstart opportunist, not a man of his word—a time-honored defense for someone who's been bested in the rough-and-tumble of business. Homer derided Sterling as a playboy indulging his literary pretensions without any practical acumen or publishing savvy. Which was kind of rich when you thought about it, given Homer's own background. No, the trouble was not what separated Sterling and Homer; it was how alike they were. Both were spoiled, handsome, charming ladies' men with a nose for writers. You might have thought they'd be natural pals, but you'd have been dead wrong. They cordially detested each other, and greatly enjoyed doing so.

Something else Sterling and Homer shared was an obsession with the poetry and person of Ida Perkins, arguably *the* representative American poet of their era. To each of them she was the embodiment of writerly—not to mention feminine—desirability. Sterling, of course, adored, revered, and published his cousin Ida; but Homer had his own attachment to her. They'd been introduced by one of Homer's writers, Giovanni Di Lorenzo, who'd had unrequited feelings of his own for Ida, and predictably enough, Homer had been dazzled by the fatally brilliant redhead. The rumor, which he was capable of putting about himself, was that they had shared their own "moment in time," as he liked to call his affairs. Nobody knew for sure, but the frequency and tenderness of Homer's allusions to Ida were an index of something for those with ears to hear. Ida, as both an attention-grabbing literary star *and* an alluring female, was a kind of Holy Grail for him, not dissimilar to, though if anything more fetishized and coveted than, "Hart, Schaffner, and Marx," as he called the leading Jewish American novelists of the late sixties, Abe Burack, Byron Hummock, and Jonathan Targoff, of whom he never managed to capture more than two at any one time, try as he might.

Authors were to Homer what paintings or real estate or jewelry were to his richer relations: living, breathing collectibles, outward and visible signs of his inward and spiritual substance. To publish Ida would in some sense be the capstone of his career, more even than Pepita, or the Three Aces, or Hart, Schaffner, and Marx, because he already owned, or had owned, all of them at one point or another, even if some had eventually managed to pry themselves loose. But Ida was the one he hadn't managed to bag, as he graciously put it. She belonged to his gnat of a rival Sterling Wainwright, who was related to her, after all, and for Homer too, blood mattered. There was simply nothing he could do about it—not that he hadn't made one frontal assault after another, only to be genteelly put off time and again. No, Ida was Homer's bird in the bush. And it rankled like an unscratched itch.

"Fucking Ida Perkins gets all the headlines and wins all the prizes, and what do we get? Bupkis!" he'd grumble, as if it was their fault, to Georges Savoy and anyone else he could buttonhole on his editorial staff, a raggle-taggle gatherum of talented misfits, many of whom he'd scooped up "on the beach," always at a considerable discount, after they'd been let go by more hard-nosed mainstream houses—starting with Frank and Georges. Each had succumbed to Homer's spell in one way or another: portly Paddy Femor, an exceptionally gifted editor whose perfectionism made it nearly impossible for him to let go of the manuscripts he noodled over, sometimes for years; cadaverous Elsa Pogorsky, known around the office as Morticia, invariably dressed in black from head to toe and forever scowling through forbidding black glasses, one of Homer's "nuns of publishing," who sat resentfully at her desk all day correcting the numberless translations of unsalable story writers and poets from the "other" Europe that Abe Burack and others were constantly pressing on Homer; crotchety, heart-of-gold copy chief Esperanza Esparza, renowned for her way with a red pencil, who seemed never to leave her desk surrounded by its array of scraggly avocado and spider plants that leached all the available light from her grimy office window.

Homer's team was united in subservient loyalty to their larger-than-life leader, whose paternal insouciance made them feel sunned-on for once in their lives: essential players in an enterprise of unquestionable significance. His allegro benevolence was like catnip. Why, it was nearly as good as money! So they beavered away while he sat back with his feet on his desk like an overdressed Tom Sawyer, smiling his toothy smile and entertaining himself placing troublemaking calls to agents and journalists.

"Who do I have to blow to get Burack's new book reviewed, baby?" he'd jaw to his sidekick Florian Brundage, affectionately known as Chowderhead, *The Daily Blade*'s chief book critic and, perhaps not entirely incidentally, a P & S novelist, picking his teeth all the while. "Your piece on that cow I'm too refined to mention, Hortense Houlihan"—to tell the truth, Homer made use of a coarser, unprintable epithet—"was shit and you know it."

Miraculously, books emerged from P & S's Augean stables. Usually they won kudos, often they won prizes, and now and again they sold reasonably well. Sometimes working for Homer was peaches and cream, occasionally it was infuriating, but mostly it was kind of fun. All you had to do was accept that it was Homer's shop, 100 percent. There were no office politics at P & S, because he decided everything. So people—those who lasted—relaxed and homed in on their work, endlessly complaining about the peremptory, ungrateful, self-involved authors whose writing they idolized. They were utterly mad, of course, but they did their level best to ignore one another's foibles since they were the same as their own. And to many of them the cramped, filthy offices on Union Square were a mind-bending, topsy-turvy little heaven on earth.

II

The Ingénue

No one, it seemed, was more in sync with Homer in his later years—with the clear exception of his longtime assistant and partner in crime, the regal Sally Savarin, uncrowned queen of the company—than Paul Dukach, the latest in the long line of editors in chief, who in the eyes of many had emerged as Homer's heir apparent.

Being number two at P & S had historically been a dangerous proposition. You couldn't win. If you were too deferential, Homer walked all over you and sooner or later lost respect for you and fired you. But if you felt the need to demonstrate your cojones—if you implied, for instance, that Eric Nielsen was "your" author—you were dead meat in a different way. Homer at the office was more than a little like Henry VIII, or maybe it was Joseph Stalin. "It's time for a change" was one of his most familiar and most dreaded nostrums, and publishing was littered with talented individuals who'd gotten the ax simply because they'd clashed with the boss. In the long run most men couldn't tolerate Homer's alpha male need to dominate; consequently, the majority of his employees were on the distaff side (the rock-bottom wages he paid could have had something to do with it, too). Homer might have thought of them as his complaisant harem, when he thought of them at all.

He was older now, though, and no longer had the same energy to stomp on the competition both inside the company and out as he once had. Paul Dukach had lucked into a sweet spot at P & S. He was unthreatening enough—"ductile" was the term one of his shrewder authors had used—that Homer could let his guard down and allow the younger man to explore his own independent editorial interests without feeling mortally threatened. To everyone's surprise, maybe Homer's most of all, they got along.

"We need to shake things up around here, Dukach," Homer would say on a Monday morning, when his vital signs were particularly healthy after a restorative weekend in the country. "It's time for a change. I think you should let Kenneally go."

Paul had recently promoted Daisy Kenneally to editor after three grueling years as his assistant, and the first book she'd acquired on her own, about the Cleveland Browns—admittedly an unusual offering for P & S; and where else in publishing would the in-house sports aficionado be a girl?—had been a surprise best seller. Out of envy, perhaps (or was it pure perversity?), Homer had unaccountably taken against her.

"I don't think we can do that, Homer," Paul would respond, as flatly as he could. "She's the most productive young editor we have."

"I think her books are thin soup. How did that novel by what's her name, Fran Drescher, do?" Homer was incorrigibly terrible with names.

"If you're referring to Nita Desser's *Plankton*, it did all right," Paul allowed, resorting to the euphemism that everyone knew meant a book had been a small, or large, disappointment.

"Well, I thought it was a dog, and the critics did, too. Woof."

Most of the time Homer grumbled and moved on. If he got you permanently fixed in his sights, though, watch out. There always seemed to be someone he was thinking of eliminating, and he'd torture him or her, the way a cat plays with a mouse. Paul knew that one big part of his job was keeping the boss distracted.

Sandy-haired, with a square-cut but receding chin, Paul wore horn-rim glasses and still looked younger than his age, which was now well into his latening thirties, though he had the incipient paunch of a sedentary man who drinks a bit too much. He'd grown up in the wilds of upstate New York—not high-end Westchester or Putnam Counties, as the city slickers thought of it, but way, way, way upstate, west of Syracuse, several hundred miles from the city. Hattersville was the Midwest, really, a rust-belt town that seemed to survive on pure inertia.

Paul had three older brothers, all obsessed if only moderately talented athletes vying for the largely withheld approval of their college football star father, now the local district court judge. To Arnold Dukach, Paul was an afterthought, the runt of the litter, and he left his youngest son's care and feeding to his harried wife, Grace—at least that was how it felt to Paul, who was close to his mother but wondered if she too might have preferred another tight end to the bookworm she'd been dealt.

As an introverted teenager desperate to escape from the rah-rah bell jar of Team Dukach, Paul had had one saving grace: Pages, the rambling, heavily stocked bookstore housed in an old brick office building on Hattersville's run-down town square where he worked afternoons and Saturdays all through high school. Morgan Dickerman, Pages' owner, was a woman of kindness and discernment, statuesque if not conventionally pretty, with prematurely graying hair; a long, elegant neck; and an assured stylishness that stood out in Hattersville, which still felt stuck in the Eisenhower era. Paul had developed a moony crush on Morgan the way adolescent boys sometimes do on their mothers' friends. He couldn't understand what someone as glamorous and sophisticated as Morgan was doing in a dump like his hometown.

She'd hailed from the actual Midwest, Des Moines, and had married Hattersville's leading (indeed, only) cardiologist, who enjoyed the godlike authority of medical men in small towns. Fifteen years into their marriage, though, Rudy Dickerman had fallen for the nurse who ran his office, and they'd divorced. Morgan, with two daughters in school, had stayed put and opened Pages. After a while, she'd formed an alliance with Ned Harman, a widower who owned the local Jeep franchise, and over time she'd made Pages into the living, breathing heart of Hattersville. People met at Pages for coffee as a matter of course, all day long. And they bought lots of books—and CDs and greeting cards and chocolate—there, too.

Morgan had taken a shine to Paul, perhaps because her own children, the younger of them a full decade older than he was, were now living in San Francisco and Hong Kong. Slowly, she'd become a kind of surrogate parent, encouraging his literary curiosity, guiding his reading, and offering a much-needed window onto the great world beyond. Paul's reliance on her was close to total, and Morgan seemed to return his affection, God knew why. He could hardly wait for Saturday to roll around so he could spend the day with her.

It was Morgan who'd first put Ida Perkins's *Striptease* into Paul's hands one November afternoon, while the rest of the Dukach tribe was watching the local Embryon

College Earwigs get trashed by Hobart and William Smith.

"Try this on for size," she said with a wink, as she turned to straighten up the children's section.

How had she known? It was love at first reading. Paul had never encountered anything so daring, so insolent, so electrically *present*, running on all cylinders at once. He'd devoured all of Ida's work, starting at the beginning with *Virgin Again* and moving all the way to her latest collection, *Arte Povera*, which had provoked yet another sensation when it had come out a few years before. Her rapturous flights in the face of convention, behavioral and literary, made Perkins's poetry thrilling; but it was the mastery, the purity of tone and timbre with which she did it, that induced Paul's amazement. On the surface, she was a flawless modern stylist; yet her unblemished instrument was employed in the service of the most unconventional thinking—as if Louis MacNeice were channeling Allen Ginsberg, or Edward Thomas the great Walt. Not since Rimbaud, Paul was sure, had a poet been so seductively subversive:

> hair
> everywhere
> clogs the drains of my dreams
> not the old flaxen tresses

the lure of your fur
is what gleams and remains
and what memory possesses

What could have been more illicitly charged for a boy who felt like an alien born into the wrong family? Poetry, particularly poetry like Ida's, has always been the lonely teenager's salvation, and Paul was entirely unoriginal in his choice of an idol when he taped her photo to his bedroom wall, like thousands of other pimply yearners before and since.

More exceptionally, over time he'd become a fanatical expert who uncovered literally everything there was to know about Ida Perkins. How her ancestors had founded Gloucester, Massachusetts, a few years after the Pilgrims made landfall at Plymouth; how her aunt Florence Perkins had served original China Trade tea to her guests in Manchester-by-the-Sea well into the 1960s; how she had been raised by her mother's sister in Springfield because of her own mother's incapacitating illness; how she'd become a dazzling heroine and subject of scandal at a very young age in an America desperate for distraction from the exigencies of war; and how over the decades she'd emerged as a national treasure, one of the icons of the age.

He also learned all about Ida's many loves, starting with her second cousin Sterling Wainwright, two and a half years her junior, when she was only eighteen and had just published her scandalous first book. And there were her marriages: to the financier Barrett Saltzman, a partner at J. P. Morgan and a family friend twenty years her senior (1945–50), then the charismatic, erratic British "Movement" poet Stephen Roentgen (1952–60), followed by Trey Turnbull, the American tenor saxophonist exiled in Paris (1961–68). From 1970 on, she'd lived in Venice with the die-hard Stalinist expat poet and literary supernova Arnold Outerbridge; and after Outerbridge's death in 1989 she'd married, in 1990, Venetian count Leonello Moro di Schiuma, the notorious collector of paintings and women, who was thirty years younger than she was, sharing his family's sixteenth-century palace on the Grand Canal.

Paul had read pretty much all there was to read about these men and their lives: not just A.O., as he was universally known, and the much-lamented Roentgen, but Turnbull and Moro, too—and how Trey's gnomic music, considered by many the most radical contribution to jazz in a generation, clashed incongruously with Moro's late-twentieth-century consumerist taste for the fashionably hideous, from Koons to Kuniyoshi, collected with an ostentation in keeping with the uncertain sources of his wealth. Paul had even delved into Ida's first marriage, to Saltzman, going as far as to examine the divorce records in the New York City archives—"irreconcilable differences," the order blandly stated. (Paul had learned somewhere that though Ida had refused a share of Saltzman's considerable wealth, he had nevertheless settled a generous annuity on her, which meant that Ida had never had to work at anything but being Ida.)

Most of all, though, he read her work, and that of her contemporary allies and competitors—even the enemies Ida had earned thanks to her unquenchable forthrightness. The English literary vamp Ora Troy, for one, had accused Ida of stealing both her bedmate Roentgen *and* the essence of her poetry, though even a casual perusal of *Ramparts of the Heart* demonstrates how time-bound and banal Ora's work is next to Ida's insuperable pyrotechnics in evoking what might superficially look like similar thematics—infidelity, religious doubt, and existential loneliness.

Ida's unimpeachably expert first book, *Virgin Again*, published by J. Laughlin at New Directions, had appeared to outraged and ecstatic notices in the little magazines, the blogs of the day, when she was an eighteen-year-old rising sophomore at Bryn Mawr. Its scabrous title had nearly gotten her expelled, but Katharine McBride, the incoming president, saw the scandal as an opportunity to demonstrate the forward thinking that had won her the job, and pardoned the young offender. Within a year there had been forty-three articles about red-hot Ida Perkins and/or *Virgin Again* in *Abrasions*, *Stalactite Review*, *The Hellions*, and numberless other magazines on both sides of the Atlantic and the Channel. Richard Aldington, to name only one, had praised the "crystalline purity" of Ida's "finger-shredding shards" in the *Camberwell Rattlebag.*

Two years later, just as the war was ending, *Ember and Icicle* was published by T. S. Eliot at Faber & Faber in London and by Laughlin in Connecticut. Eliot wrote Marianne Moore, whose own revolutionary work he had championed two decades previously, "Young Miss Perkins, like you before her, has helped recalibrate my understanding of my origins," while Moore herself told Ida, "We are pierced by the intricate needlework of your asperitic formulations." She had the obligatory meeting with Miss Moore on the same bench outside the New York Public Library where the senior poet had met her soon-to-be disciple Elizabeth Bishop, though little seems to have come of their encounter, as far as Paul or anyone else could tell from the available evidence, which included Mollie Macdonald's scathing cameo portrait of Ida as the promiscuous villainess of *The Bridge Game*, her satire of Seven Sisters womanhood. Neither Moore nor Bishop seems to have had much truck with Ida—and, perhaps unsurprisingly, she turns up nowhere in Bishop's voluminous correspondence.

And Ida? She herself said very little; at least Paul could discover very little she'd said. Unlike most of the garrulous scribblers of her moment, she blazed across her world silently, cunningly, her only documented words the ones stamped on the smoking pages of her Faber and ND books—though Sterling succeeded in wooing her over to Impetus as soon as he was able. Apart, that is, from a few barbed remarks caught on the fly (or could they have been manufactured ex post facto?) by the literary memoirists of her era. Millicent Crabtree, in her recollections of life with Sheldon Storm, reported that Ida refused to spend the night in the composer's weekend house in the Berkshires. "I don't trust men with fingers that fast," she is supposed to have complained, insisting on bunking in at a nearby rooming house. She also reportedly told an openmouthed Delmore Schwartz, who up till then had been in hot and voluble pursuit, "Hold your tongue, please, if you want me to hold your prick."

Was Ida what they used to call a "man's woman," with not a lot of time for her sisters in the art? Paul thought it was possible. "Your aloofness and frivolity leave me arrested and . . . chilled," Moore wrote on February 15, 1944, after one of their rare meetings, giving Ida the title for her third book, as it turned out. *Aloofness and Frivolity* was published in 1947, its modernist severity and private preoccupations—"navel-gazing," more than one critic sniffed—seemingly at a far remove from America's triumphalist postwar mood.

Not that Ida appeared to care. The structure and organizing principles of her first mature period were already well established. Stark dichotomies, rigid caesuras, and the same dissonances that make modernist music so challenging to the conventional ear were the stuff of her art in the forties and early fifties. Nevertheless, her freshness and informality put her at odds with her contemporaries and competitors, among them the neo-Miltonic Robert Lowell (also a relation, on her mother's side) and the willfully obscure, surrealist early Bishop. Ida's love poems—and all her poems were arguably love poems, from first to last—are defined by contrast and dichotomy, the yin and yang of lover and loved one, giver and taker, remover and removed, night and day, growth and decay. A world of ineluctable oppositions with no gray areas: that is early Ida Perkins to a T.

It wasn't long before Ida was almost universally acclaimed as the distinctive poetic voice of her generation, though no one could have predicted the broad popularity she would later find. Yet in spite of the standoffishness for which she was often criticized, Paul perceived that Ida's passions were accessible to everyone on paper from the very beginning—except in her "atonal" period in the early eighties, when she experimented (uncomfortably, most would say) with poetic abstraction. Nothing is hidden or remote in Ida Perkins; it's all on the surface, in your face—the title of her epochal fourth book, which was quoted and imitated by Lowell, Duncan, Plath, and Gunn, among others. Lapidary—obsidian, even—the poems nevertheless embody human feeling with a directness that over time proved irresistible for hundreds of thousands of readers. Paul saw, too, that some of these poets' most characteristic lines had been lifted from Ida. Think "Viciousness in the kitchen!" (though Ida was rarely known to cook a meal), or "savage servility," or "The love of old men is not worth a lot," or even "Life, friends, is boring." Then think again. Yes, Ida was there first.

But everyone—or almost everyone—stole from her. Paul discerned her influence in her snubbed suitor Delmore Schwartz, in the plangency of later Roethke, everywhere in Rukeyser, and in Elspeth Adams's mid-period figured love lyrics—though nowhere, as we've seen (the silence is deafening), in Bishop. Ida was one of those rare poets who bridge the divide between aesthetic schools. The Beats and Objectivists looked to her every bit as much as the East Coast formalists. The fountainhead, the freewheeling, free-spirited Martha Graham of mid-century poetry, its Barefoot Contessa, with a dash of Dorothy Parkerish spice for good measure, she was ages ahead of everyone, and the living, breathing antidote to everything she'd come from. Like Botticelli's Venus, she arrived out of nowhere on a half shell to bring up the rear of modernism. Quoting her is inevitable, somehow: *Bringing Up the Rear* was Ida's arguably most influential collection, the one that finally brought her diva status—and reliable royalties.

Thanks to Ida, too, poetry not infrequently found itself at the heart of American culture and society. Paul considered her encounter with Jacqueline Kennedy at the 1962 White House dinner for French culture minister and all-around culture hero André Malraux the stuff of myth. Malraux was seated on Jackie's right, of course, but few were aware that Ida was on *his* right and that he spent virtually the entire evening in tête-à-tête conversation with her (Paul learned that she had been ably translated into French, practically from the beginning, by the critic René Schorr's first wife, Renée, an intimate of Malraux's). For most of the dinner, Jackie was left staring into space, pulling her Parker House roll to bits. Needless to say, Ida never darkened the White House door again during the Kennedys' tragically brief reign—though she was later close to both Rosalynn and Nancy, to the surprise of many, and a kind of fairy godmother to Chelsea, who stayed with her twice in Venice, complete with Secret Service detail, during her father's second term, when she needed a break from Monicagate.

In the sixties, Ida progressed from literary superstar to celebrity, pure and simple. The transition had something to do, no doubt, with the simplifying and opening up of her work, which gradually lost its hard edge and became readable for everyone, while losing none of its depth and originality. (Could it have been due to the influence of Trey Turnbull? Paul wondered; or had her renown encouraged Ida to relax and clarify, though she was constitutionally incapable of dumbing down?) Her popularity also had to do, he could see, with her natural beauty, her penchant for risk-taking, and, above all, her well-known talent for love.

There was grumbling among her jealous "peers," of course—what else do poets do but complain about each other's success, both critical and erotic? Who was it who said the reason there's so much backbiting among poets is because there's so little at stake? Ida had been the exception that proved the rule. By then, she'd moved into a region of fame that left virtually every other writer of any stripe in the dust. Forget *The Hudson Review* and *Poetry*. Now *Time*, *Fortune*, *Ladies' Home Journal*, *US News & World Report*, *Saturday Review*, *The New Yorker*—even *Reader's Digest*—were desperate to write about and interview and publish her. Her "What Becomes a Legend Most" Blackglama ad—lustrous sable over a brown tweed Chanel suit and oxfords—was a sensation. A vampish, guileless Meryl Streep with flaming red hair—that was Ida in her late thirties.

Her occasional stealth appearances in New York and San Francisco in those years were widely reported on—and, as Paul discovered, occasionally invented. When Janis Joplin sang "Marginal Discharge" at Woodstock, Ida was reputedly sighted in the audience, though this may have been a desperate fan's acid-stoked fantasy. Carly Simon and Carole King recorded a duet version of "Broken Man," Ida's sexiest, most unforgettable song, which went platinum in 1970 (that's Ida shaking the tambourine in the background):

Broken man,
you're just skin and bone,
broken-down man,
like I'm skin and bone.
Broken man,
why can't I leave you alone?

Take my heart
and you torture me.
Break my heart,
I'm in misery.
Broken man,
will we ever be free?

Paul, though, preferred the version on Turnbull's Grammy-winning album *The Ida Sessions*, on which she recites a dozen of her best-loved lyrics, filigreed with Trey's smoking riffs on tenor saxophone.

In the seventies, during her short-lived flirtation with Maoism, when her work turned strident in the eyes of many, Ida was the only person ever to appear simultaneously on the covers of *Rolling Stone*, *Tel Quel*, and *Interview*. By then, though, she'd reunited with the leonine Outerbridge, now a virtual outcast as an unrepentant Stalinist, whom she'd met in London a decade earlier. Soon she more or less disappeared into the nimbus of A.O.'s Venetian silence (he'd long since stopped publishing). Ida kept writing, but her work, too, turned inward, though her crossover popularity with baby boomers had undeniable staying power over the next three decades. A new book would emerge every two or three years as if dropped from the heavens, and Sterling would gather it up and publish it at Impetus to general stupefaction and acclaim. Ida slowly became an off-site legend, a great hovering absent presence. Which only whetted the appetite of her fan base, who remained passionately loyal even as they themselves turned middle-aged.

Paul knew it all, from Ida's first tentative poems in the *Chestnut Hill Herbivore*, already pregnant with intimations of future significance, to the most exquisite Swiss plaquettes of the fifties and sixties, published in gilt-edged, snakeskin-bound editions of no more than twenty or thirty. While still in Hattersville he quietly became a—no, *the*—leading connoisseur of Perkinsiana; it was his secret hoard of adoration, the way model cars or baseball cards are for other kids. Paul let his classmates deify Magic Johnson and Kurt Cobain; his obsession with Ida Perkins made her his and his alone in a way no one who was flesh and blood ever could be. And he guarded his heroine jealously—though he couldn't help crowing about some of his discoveries to Morgan, who was mind-boggled by his maniacal fixation on his one-and-only poet.

"What did I start here? There *are* other writers, Paul,"

she'd admonish him, rolling her eyes. "There's Eliot, or Faulkner, or Stevens, or even the misunderstood Emily D. Hell, there's even Arnold Outerbridge."

Paul would just shake his head. Every word of Ida's was pure gold. No one else could come anywhere near her.

Word slowly got out in scholarly circles that an oddball boy in Hattersville, New York, was the go-to guy about the elusive Ida, and over time Paul was inundated by bibliographical and biographical, even interpretive, queries from graduate students and eventually from established scholars of modernism. "What is all this strange mail you're getting, Paul?" Grace Dukach would ask her son suspiciously, shrugging with incomprehension when he showed her the letters from English departments at Purdue and Baylor and Yale.

He'd even had a less-than-pleasant exchange with Elliott Blossom, critical poobah and self-styled kingmaker among contemporary poets. Blossom had written in *The Covering Cherub* that the "cyclamen stains" in "Attis," the central text in Ida's incendiary 1970 collection, *Remove from the Right*, referred to blood spilled in the Vietnam War. Paul, though, had pointed out, in a letter to the editor of the *Cherub* that has since become cherished academic lore, that the phrase occurs twice elsewhere in her work: in the little-known early poem "Verga," of 1943, and in "Nice Weather," an uncollected prose text from the late fifties, where it describes a pool of dried semen on her sleeping lover's thigh (reputedly Harry Mathews's). Blossom had withdrawn in high dudgeon and Paul understood that his chances for a university career had dwindled to almost nothing.

Which was fine with him, because what he wanted, he'd come to understand, was to be involved with the writers of his own generation who were going to be Ida's heirs, even if he couldn't imagine being one of them himself. At Morgan's urging, he'd gotten himself south to NYU (and NYC!) for college, where he unimaginatively majored in English, edited the literary magazine, and more or less lived in the Bobst Library on Washington Square. He landed a student job in the manuscript collection after classes and during summer vacations, and on his lunch breaks he haunted the Strand and the other used-book stores on Fourth Avenue, most of them soon to be killed off by the Internet.

He'd also fallen under the spell of the rail-thin poet/critic Evan Halpern, whose view of Ida was more tempered than Paul's, and who enjoyed winding him up about his obsession.

"I'm afraid Ida Perkins doesn't come within striking distance of Elspeth Adams, Paul," Evan would attack, pitting Paul's most beloved NYU teacher against his deepest admiration, and preparing for the barrage he knew would be forthcoming from his young disciple. "She has none of her finesse, none of her historical ballast."

"You're just trying to get me riled," Paul would volley back. "You know how I feel about Miss Adams. She's the best teacher I'll ever have"—he'd grin defiantly at Evan as he said this—"and an unforgettable poet. But she just doesn't have Ida's daring and reach and joie de vivre. She's so careful and depressive . . . and . . . and closeted. She never has any fun—at least not on paper. She's always the unloved lover, the loser, the waif. Ida is so up front and open about everything. And she knows how to enjoy herself, too."

"Precisely. No implication, no tragic subtext. She's a flat, declarative open book, always engaged and engorged. She's a monotone ecstatic bore."

Paul secretly enjoyed the way his teacher teased him about his attachment, but he was nowhere near ready to admit to anyone, least of all to Evan, that Ida was less than perfection. He was far too invested in his investment to submit it to any kind of test. He did, however, take Evan's advice and write his undergraduate thesis on someone else: he'd chosen Arnold Outerbridge, concentrating on the influence of his postwar work on Ida.

At NYU Paul had also slowly, painfully, begun to accept that he liked boys better than girls, and had lived through a series of infatuations that brought him moments of intense joy but more often a misery he experienced as a low-grade fever he couldn't kick. Ted Curtis, a fellow student in Evan's symbolist poetry class, had been Paul's first serious crush. A taciturn blond from Reading, Pennsylvania, Ted was certifiably heterosexual yet desperately in need of positive reinforcement. Paul's not truly returned yet never fully rejected attraction consumed them both through college, until Ted went off to law school at Berkeley and they lost touch.

Love in the flesh remained elusive. It drew yet frightened him. This was the late eighties, after all, the most terrifying days of the plague. Surrounded everywhere by insolent youth and beauty, Paul looked and lusted but didn't dare touch.

As graduation neared, he became more and more worried about what he was going to do with his life. Terror gripped him that he'd have to go back to his family in Hattersville, a living death. After a series of panicked consultations with Morgan, he decided he'd give publishing a try, since it had to do with books and writers, the only things he'd ever cared about. Morgan, who, Paul had come to understand, was one of the most respected booksellers in the country, arranged an interview with her friend Homer Stern, the premier literary publisher of his generation, as she described him to Paul. "He's an outrageous cad," she told him, with a knowing glint in her eye. "But he'll teach you more about publishing in one day than you'll ever learn anywhere else."

Homer had been all bluster and grand gesture when Paul paid him a visit, but, alas, he had no openings. It happened, though, that he knew about a position in the rights department at Howland, Wolff, and before long Paul found himself a member of the workforce, pulling down $300 a week and as many free books as he could haul home to his rabbit hutch of a studio in Chelsea.

His generally sunny demeanor, largely adopted in imitation of Morgan, which he managed to project even when he didn't feel sunny, along with his judgment, which turned out to be usually sound thanks to Evan's training and his voluminous reading, earned him Dan Wolff's and Larry Friedman's confidence, and after a couple of years he'd been elevated to junior editor at HW. But P & S remained his ideal.

True, they had legendarily disgusting quarters on Union Square, the city's major needle park, and rock-bottom wages; but the quasi-religious fealty Homer inspired in his crew was a siren call to Paul. That and the authors! Not just scary Pepita Erskine, perfectionist Iain Spofford, and hypercool Thor Foxx, but the haunting young E. C. Benton, who'd sprung like Athena from the mountains of Carolina; or Grenada Brooks, the hope of Caribbean literature; or Dmitry Chavchavadze, the larger-than-life Georgian poet; and Australian Padraic Snell; and St. John Vezey, South Africa's national bard, and . . . and . . . and . . . The list was practically endless. There was something about its homemade, familial—or was it paternalistic?—feeling for writers that made the shabby-chic firm fatally appealing to Paul. Each of their books was a sacred object. Paul was in love with Caroline Koblenz's elegant jackets and typography that paid subtle homage to the work of W. A. Dwiggins, the genius behind Knopf's magisterial bindings and settings, which had long ago set a never-to-be-equaled standard in book design. He loved the heft of the books in his hand. He loved the colors of their bindings. He loved how they smelled.

A few years later, after he had worked with a number of presentable if far from immortal novelists and journalists at HW, there had at last been an opening in Homer's editorial department and, with yet another assist from Morgan, Paul had been able to make the leap. Homer took him out for a ceremonial lunch at his daily watering hole, the Soft-shell Crab, where they each downed a shot of vodka followed by the Crab's popular wasabi tuna burgers. Paul reported for work two weeks later.

III

Home at Last

Paul had felt at home the moment he'd walked into the boxed-in, ill-lit P & S lobby. The place looked more like his idea of the offices of a porn magazine (there seemed to be one upstairs, down the hall from the rehab center on the eighth floor) than a temple of contemporary literature. A broken couch and frosted glass dividers fought for attention with certificates for the National Book Awards, Pulitzer Prizes, and National Book Critics Circle Awards won by house authors appended helter-skelter over the receptionist's rickety desk alongside less prepossessing announcements, like the American Book Designers Federation 1969 honorable mention for typography. P & S specialized in Nobel Prizes, in fact, but there were no plaques for them, just the gold medals that Paul had noticed on Homer's desk during their interviews. Later that morning, he was given a cubicle on the south side of the hallway (Homer had called it "a nice office with a window" at lunch), equipped with a boxy Korean computer console and a telephone, both of which appeared to be in working order.

Manuscripts from literary agents would show up in neat

gray or powder-blue boxes on his pockmarked old school desk, or in battered manila envelopes if they were coming from writers without representation, and he'd read through them with the requisite show-me detachment. In 90 percent of cases, you could tell within a page or two whether the writer could write. Ninety percent of the time, box or no box, he or she could not. Every so often, though, the words would cohere, the sentences would follow one on another with lockstep plausibility, and Paul would begin to feel an unsettling combination of elation and fear—elation at the linguistic and psychological aptness of what he was reading, and fear, as he went on, that this undeniably gifted writer would veer off and spoil her creation before he could finish the stack of pages.

When, miraculously, the work was actually fine, Paul would run into Homer's office half crazed with excitement, shouting, "We have to do this!" Which, remarkably enough in Paul's experience, was music to Homer's ears. "Go, go, go, baby!" he'd shout back, as if cheering on a two-year-old at the track. Paul would hondle, as Homer put it, with the writer's agent over the advance—usually no more than $25,000 or $30,000 in those days—and often enough, mirabile dictu, the manuscript, and its author, would be theirs to coax and hover over and massage into a living, breathing printed and bound novel or book of stories or poems or essays or work of reportage that could be trumpeted to booksellers and reviewers and that increasingly endangered species, the retail book buyer, as something not to be missed.

Many P & S books turned out to be a bit more "specialized"—or should we say Impetus-like?—than was generally appreciated. Paul subscribed to the saw of Larry Friedman at Howland, Wolff that a publisher could either lead public taste or run after it. He wanted to lead, to introduce new voices, to make the common reader a little less common, which was the firm's stated mission, after all; but sometimes he got tired of hearing how difficult their books were to sell from the travelers, a group of hard-boiled, hard-drinking commission salesmen and -women, old-timers who at heart were as devoted to good books as anyone in the office, if not more so, but who had to make a buck, as did Homer and Co.—though the editors often seemed unaware that this was a fundamental aspect of their work. So the sales and marketing departments, under cool, super-competent Maureen Rinaldi and market-wise Seth Berle, who seemed like different species but functioned beautifully together in spite or because of it, would tart up the new Brooks or Burns or Burack with a stunning jacket and an only mildly misleading tagline and pass it off as far more easy to digest than it actually was. Paul would sometimes mutter, not too loudly, that it was P & S's job to put over a few good books on the unsuspecting public—not that they were fooled all that often.

Still, in his years at the firm he and his fellow editors had managed to discover a number of writers who had developed into an identifiable group, indeed almost a generation of their own, who had made a notable cultural contribution *and* were sought after by readers. George Howe Nough's *Nightshade;* Julian Entrekin's *Subtle Specimens;* Nita Desser's breakout second novel, *Mud Rambling;* and Eric Nielsen's *Show Me the Mountain* were books that went a long way toward defining the aesthetic and the preoccupations of their moment. Nielsen and Entrekin in particular had become enormous best sellers and major prizewinners (Paul sometimes referred to them around the office as "Hemingway and Fitzgerald") and Nielsen, with his fourth novel, *The Insolent Hours*—Paul was particularly chuffed that he'd come up with the title—had emerged as the novelist of the moment.

What Paul loved best was working with the authors on their texts. Some manuscripts—the ultimate rarities—showed up on his desk virtually letter-perfect and simply needed to be printed, but most called for pruning, or even sometimes having an extra limb or two lopped off. Some writers wanted their hand held as their book developed year after year—though over and over he had watched them learn to write their books by . . . writing them; by the time they'd got to the end, they recognized that what had to be done was to go back to the beginning and recast the first half in the light of what had come together in the second. And some simply wanted to bask in the sunlight of his approval. What the great Pepita Erskine really loved was sitting at the long table in Paul's office and going over her manuscript with him, word by word. She radiated joy at his undivided but critical attention, and Paul himself never felt more wanted or appreciated than during their chaste lovefests. The fact that she could walk past him in the square the next day without recognizing him hardly mattered.

Over the decade, book by book, season by season, Paul and Daisy Kenneally and Maureen and Seth et al. had managed to extend the company's literary franchise for a new generation. Paul would call Morgan every now and then and tell her about the incredible manuscripts he'd read and sometimes even acquired, or the bullets he'd dodged, or the masterpieces that had heartbreakingly gotten away—and about his boss's day-in-day-out outrageousness.

"You won't believe what Homer did last night!" he'd dish. "He called Tim Tudow"—a top-notch if not exactly top-flight Hollywood-style literary agent with an unwavering Cheshire cat smile—"a 'toothpaste salesman.' To his face!"

Morgan would listen with the requisite beguilement or outrage when he recounted the internecine squabbles, the gossip, the good old low-down fun that made P & S—and publishing—so enjoyable. She'd snort at the amorous entanglements of Paul's fellow workers, or the underhanded tactics of their competitors and the outrageous advances they had been willing to pay—as high as $100,000 for a first novel!—or the outlandish fights Homer would pick with other publishers, whom he was only too happy to sound off about publicly to anyone who would listen, especially if he or she happened to work for a major newspaper.

"Music to my ears," she'd croon in her blue-sky Iowa accent, taking another late-night sip of Chardonnay during their phoned-in drinks date. "The human comedy! It's keeping me young."

For Paul, like many of his fellows, the company had turned out to be a haven in a heartless world. His work was his life, apart from an occasional fling that went nowhere. Many of the writers he'd idolized as a student were house authors, and some of them had now become "his," their previous editors having retired or moved on to higher-paying jobs elsewhere. Everyone understood that any author with any kind of profile was automatically the personal property of Homer. Nevertheless, Pepita Erskine and Orin Roden and all the women's heartthrob, the divine Padraic Snell, took Paul's calls and had errands for him to run, and he'd been thrilled to run them. Until, in the eyes of many in the tight-knit community of agents and writers and journalists and other editors, Paul and P & S had become more or less synonymous. Recognizing which, as he lay awake on his sagging daybed wedged in between the stacks of books and galleys and manuscripts in his West Nineteenth Street walk-up, he would sometimes shake his head in grateful wonder.

Still, the writer Paul cared most about, the ever-incandescent Ida Perkins—"the bitch that got away," Homer would mutter when he was feeling competitive and resentful, which he did whenever he wasn't feeling triumphant—was nowhere near Union Square. Paul looked on in envy while she racked up prizes all over the world, appeared on *Charlie Rose* and Bill Moyers's shows and even, one unforgettable January afternoon, for a full hour on *Oprah*, gave sell-out readings at the biggest venues, appeared in the gossip columns with her fancy acquaintances, and sold an outlandish number of books for a poet. And as he watched it all, book after book, year after year, he felt the unassuageable ache of unrequited passion transmute into bittersweet longing. He and Ida were like an old couple by now; they'd been through a lot together, and they would always be each other's—if only in his head.

He'd experienced a more immediate kind of pain around Elspeth Adams when he'd been a student in her poetry workshop at NYU, so overwhelmed with love and insufficiency he'd been virtually speechless. Being in her presence, when he'd gotten to know her, had been so much what he wanted that he couldn't enjoy it; he was literally sick with reverence. He'd get a stomach ache when he was invited to Miss Adams's apartment for dinner. She was a grandmotherly figure, richly if soberly dressed, without pretension but with the quiet dignity of someone who knew her worth. She insisted on calling her students by their last names; to her, he was "Mr. Dukach" and she was "Miss Adams"—no ersatz "Ms." for her. Paul loved this, like everything else about her. He was enchanted by the purr of her smoke-enriched voice, her lowball rapier irony, her politely expressed disdain for everything noisy and showy about her contemporaries. Poets like Audrey Dienstfrey, who performed for rapt audiences with a rock band for backup, moaning incantations about the vicissitudes of her genitalia, were anathema to Miss Adams, though it was a nearly open secret that she'd had a series of rocky affairs with younger women. She had one of the steeliest intelligences he had ever encountered. Her sense of herself, of her womanhood, was multilayered, not easy to parse.

He'd last seen her when he was still at HW, at the Modern Language Association convention in New York. John Adams (no relation) had premiered his "Starlight" song cycle based on a group of wonderful poems from her Pulitzer Prize–winning collection, *Intergalactica*, sung by the ethereal Viridiana Bruck. A few months later, aged sixty-six, she'd had a heart attack and died alone in her apartment overlooking the Brooklyn Heights Promenade.

Her suddenly expanded circle of intimates referred to Elspeth by her given name now that she was gone, but Paul hesitated before saying it when, to his amazement, he'd become the editor responsible for her work, once Georges Savoy had finally retired. He felt an intense loyalty and responsibility to Miss Adams and her work, though he had always considered Ida a more ambitious and more adventurous writer. He cherished Miss Adams's letters to him, which he kept in his copy of her *Collected Poems*, the binding of which was in danger of giving out, and he'd hung her photograph next to Ida's above the desk in his apartment.

As he grew into his life at work, though, Paul found he had gradually lost a degree of the awe for the writers he worked with. They no longer left him tongue-tied, though their talent often still amazed him. Eventually, Miss Adams had had to become Elspeth to Paul, too. You couldn't work with someone for too long, even if she was gone, without somehow ending up on a first-name basis. He'd come to appreciate that writers were just like everyone else, except when they were more so. It sometimes seemed that they'd been able to develop their gifts thanks to a lack of inhibition, an inner permission to feel and react, that made them seem self-absorbed and insensitive to the existence of anyone else.

Pepita Erskine was a prime example. She'd grown up black and dirt-poor in Detroit, but by dint of her brilliance and courage and strength of personality, she'd made herself into an intellectual and moral force to be reckoned with, even as a very young woman. She'd driven cross-country to New York after a noisy career at Berkeley, where she'd been a thorn in the side of radical student leader Ronnie Morrone, whom she'd accurately called out as both racist and sexist, and had gone on to make her mark nationally as a counterculture columnist at *The Daily Blade.*

In excoriating the self-congratulatory liberal clerisy, Pepita had refused with remarkable success to be labeled a black or a woman writer, or a left-winger, or a sexual renegade. She was also an indefatigable culture vulture, hoovering up every civilizing tidbit she could get her hands on—poetry, literary theory, dance, music, theater, film. She was an insatiable maw of desire and need to know, to experience, to opine. And her insatiability extended to the creators themselves, for Pepita had boundary issues. Approbation, in someone as constitutionally critical as she, often got confused with passion, and her affairs with the writers, dancers, and artists she looked up to were widely known. Paul referred to them as her "seminars"—private sessions with the masters in their fields, held at their feet and sometimes in their beds. Men or women, it made no difference to Pepita, as long as her chosen objects could give her a run for her formidable mental money and momentarily assuage her need for recognition and response. She was literally enamored with art—arguably less so with the individuals who created it, who often turned out to have inconvenient needs and egos of their own, which on occasion dwarfed even hers.

Homer always referred to Pepita as Pootie. He had nicknames for many of his current favorite—or unfavorite—allies or antagonists. (Sometimes it was hard to tell the difference.) The Nympho, the Dauphin, the Dwarf, and the Slightly Used Canadian, whatever that meant, were only some of the characters in the eternal soap opera that was publishing for him.

One day Paul got up the courage to ask him, "Why do you call Pepita Pootie, Homer?" To which he answered matter-of-factly, "Because she's such a sweet little pootie-tat."

Right. Of the attributes that could be assigned to Pepita—brilliance, originality, courage, stridency, arrogance, neediness, narcissism—sweetness was not first among them. Indeed, her nickname around the office, "the Purring P," told you everything you needed to know about her relations with the staff. Homer's moniker showed that he had been on the receiving end of Pepita's cat's—or bear's—paw often enough; indeed, it was clear to one and all that she had him in her thrall.

After all, it was Pepita' s voice—insolent, belabored with Germanic Seriousness, lightened and enlivened by a dash of jive, and insistent on its own unimpeachability—that had become the hallmark of P & S style. At a critical point in its history, Pepita's intellectual reach and tropism for controversy had lent the house an aura of urgent cultural significance that it had never lost. Pepita Erskine, the scourge of white liberalism, had become white liberalism's dangerous darling—and the quintessential P & S author. She certainly thought so, and Homer concurred, and they had a correspondingly intense relationship—part father-daughter, part professional, part flirtatious (Paul had heard they'd been lovers; he couldn't be sure, but he knew that for Homer no complicated relationship with a woman could fail to be sexual in some sense)—and 100 percent transactional.

Paul remembered how, long before he'd worked for Homer, he'd run into him lunching with Pepita in the old restaurant at One Fifth Avenue. They were sitting side by side, wearing matching leather jackets and exuding a bonhomie that felt faintly postcoital to Paul. Glamorous Meredith Gethers, the agent who was Paul's date that day, brought him over to their banquette to say hello. Homer was civil, just barely, but when Meredith started to commiserate about the *Daily Blade*'s scathing review of her client Earl Burns's new novel, he cut her off. "It's a fart in the wind," he sneered with a dismissive wave, before turning back to the real object of his interest.

One of Pepita's most notable seminars had been with Dmitry Chavchavadze, the émigré Georgian poet. The fact that he lived in Atlanta, where he held an endowed chair at Emory University, confused matters, for people were often unsure which kind of Georgian he was. On his arrival in New York in 1982 after being expelled from Brezhnev's Soviet Union, Dmitry had been lionized by Manhattan's glitterati, until they bumped up against his hard-line rightist politics, by which time it was too late. Before you could say *Bozhe moi*, Pepita and Dmitry had become inseparable.

Pepita, who had a gorgeous ebony complexion set off with cherry-red lipstick and a high-teased Afro, dressed like a Seven Sisters coed of yesteryear in flared corduroy skirts and penny loafers, while Dmitry, with his soul patch and filled-out figure, looked like what he was, an aging émigré intellectual on the dole in America's groves of academe. Their seminar lasted only a few months, for in Dmitry, Pepita's ego had more than met its steely match. Paul used to say that you didn't get to be Dmitry Chavchavadze or Pepita Erskine by being nice (her war with Susan Sontag over the black characters in Jean Genet's dramas had gone practically nuclear). But Dmitry, with his unmovable detestation of Communism, his intransigent commitment to poetic formalism, and his bludgeoning disdain for his intellectual inferiors, took the cake.

Dmitry's hatred of his Soviet tormentors meant that he approved of all anti-Communists, first among them Ronald Reagan, and considered left-leaners "dangerous fools"—and it was during their short-lived liaison that Pepita's notorious rightward shift had begun. From the hammer-and-tongs opponent of midcult conformism of her early essays, she reemerged in her later years as a defender of the much-maligned and soon-to-disappear literary canon, the ultimate Great Books girl she'd once been in Black Bottom, where, as a bucktoothed teenager, she'd inhaled volume after volume of the Modern Library.

Dmitry was considered the most important Georgian poet of the century, and the Swedish Academy had concurred, enNobeling him unprecedentedly early, at the age of thirty-eight. His poems in Russian were said to be at once hypnotically lyrical and cynically disaffected, but some saw the English-language versions, which he insisted on creating himself, as an unintentional pastiche that relied on an insufficient understanding of his target language. Still, his status as a freedom fighter combined with his brilliance and take-no-prisoners implacability conferred impregnable authority on Dmitry. "Is sheet!" he'd shout, about the work of a writer he didn't rate, which was most of them. "Sheet! Sheet! Sheet!!" This turned out to be a surefire argumentative technique, since few had the temerity to disagree—except, on occasion, the fearless Pepita. And their relationship came a cropper over . . . who else but Ida Perkins?

Dmitry had met Ida and A.O. in Venice soon after he'd been expelled from the Soviet Union. Needless to say, he had nothing but contempt for Outerbridge, whom he derided as an apologist for the worst criminal in modern history. So their encounter, as one might have expected, had not gone well. Homer's cousin Celine Mannheim, the modernist collector, who was Arnold's landlady in Venice—he and Ida lived in a flat that looked over Celine's luxuriant garden on Dorsoduro—had given a reception in honor of Dmitry's arrival and had been shocked to come upon her glamorous new social trophy making a scene, insulting her tenant in her own salon. Ida, needless to say, had been outraged, and she'd gone on the record about it. "Georgian Honor," her scathing takedown of Dmitry's Stalinist anti-Stalinism, had occasioned the longest-running exchange of letters in the history of *The Protagonist*, the savage old-left review. Pepita, to the surprise of many, had taken Arnold's (and Ida's) part, and this had proven intolerable for Dmitry.

"Mr. Chavchavadze, for all his political shrewdness, has failed to take on board Arnold Outerbridge's vital role in denouncing the defensive Babbittry of prewar American society, and the promise of an alternative, however eventually disillusioning, that the Soviet Union once held out," Pepita wrote in the fifth *réplique* of her fourteen-letter exchange with Dmitry, which was to prove fatal to their relationship.

"They're all alike," he'd been heard to mutter after breaking off their increasingly bitter dialogue—though he left it unspecified who precisely "they" were: Americans, writers, fellow-traveling socialist roaders, women, blacks? It could have been any or all.

Still, Pepita and Dmitry, together or apart, were always and only themselves. Pepita knew what she knew, and brooked no disagreement. But Dmitry was her match, a monument to the egoism of the transcendentally gifted. They were insufferable, both of them, to each other as much as to anyone else—maybe even to themselves, once in a blue moon. Yet, like Pepita, Dmitry, despite his dagger goatee and rotund belly, had undeniable charisma. Even his put-downs of other poets—except for Snell and Vezey, Homer's other Aces, who were automatically exempted—were delicious. Dmitry knew he was bad, and there was a twinkle in his eye when he was at his most obstreperous, as if he was sharing a joke with you: the joke of his own outrageousness.

"Publishing would be so wonderful without those wretched authors," one of Homer's disenchanted colleagues once complained. Not for Paul. He floated on a sea of entrancement, pistol-whipped by the vagaries of his writers' oversize neediness and self-absorption yet buoyed by the rewards of helping their work see the light of day. He, who was so beset by doubt—about his own talents, his eligibility for love, his capacity for happiness—never for a minute questioned the value of what he was doing. He was made for it, and he knew it. So he kept his head down, at one with his work, while his life flew by.

IV

The World of Sterling Wainwright

Paul met Sterling Wainwright, who at seventy-eight was beginning to bend more than a bit, at an Impetus New Poets reading at the New School seven or eight years into his tenure at P & S, in the fall of 2005. With his ubiquitous pipe and slightly threadbare gentility, Sterling exuded a patrician ease and impersonal openness that the younger man found enthralling, if a bit intimidating.

"Come and see me," Sterling had offered, but Paul, who was shy with people he looked up to, had been slow to respond. When he'd mustered the gumption to call, they'd met at the Cornelia Street Café one afternoon for iced tea, and then repaired to Sterling's apartment on Barrow Street for something stronger. They'd talked shop for hours: poetry, translators, the history of Impetus, and endless other topics, and Paul had emerged fascinated with Sterling himself—so offhand, so experienced, such a humble brag, as Paul called people who affected modesty, all the while letting you know just how accomplished they were.

And Sterling seemed to take an interest in Paul, too,

gratified that someone from the younger generation knew enough to appreciate what he and his crowd had been up to in their salad days. Sterling had a need to testify, to transmit his lore and wisdom, and he professed to be stunned by the depth of Paul's knowledge of Ida and her work. He gave the impression that he'd found in Paul the faithful receiver and disciple he'd been waiting for.

Sterling suggested that he and Paul keep talking, so every couple of weeks Paul showed up for another round of stories about Outerbridge, Ida, and the rest of Sterling's writers, so different from Homer's, yet equally impressive in their rarefied concentration on the most experimental practitioners of modernism. Slowly, a camaraderie developed. Paul, whose capacity for hero worship was bottomless, became attached to the older man. Sterling could feel it, Paul was sure, and basked in his young friend's admiration. The fact that Paul worked for one of Sterling's professional foes only seemed to increase his appeal in Sterling's eyes.

The antipathy between Homer and Sterling was toxic. Paul was used to Homer's talking Sterling and Impetus down, having heard about their author-related dustups over the years. They were still fighting, even now, over who should publish Giovanni Di Lorenzo's letters. Paul had turned down Di Lorenzo's weak later poems and stories and Di Lorenzo had taken them to Impetus, but his widow had recently collared Homer at a party and implored him to publish Giovanni's literary remains. Homer, who could be a surprisingly soft touch where wives and daughters were concerned, felt a sentimental obligation to do so, bolstered no doubt by Sterling's involvement. They had sparred over early Targoff, too, and mid-period Roden. Paul, though, always felt Ida was humming somewhere in the background.

When Paul let it drop that he'd met Sterling, Homer had been grandly condescending.

"I hadn't realized he was still working. Not that he ever did." Homer tapped his hand languidly over his mouth in imitation of a yawn. "Sterling Wainwright is a dollar-a-year man if I've ever seen one."

"Impetus seems to be going strong, better than ever," Paul countered mildly.

"Name their last best seller. I hear Wainwright spends all his time upstate. God, I wish he'd roll over so I could put my hand on Ida Perkins's thigh." Homer's yawn exploded into a guffaw.

Paul got reciprocal static from Sterling.

"How's Homer?" he'd ask Paul whenever they got together, his question anything but innocent. For Sterling, Homer epitomized everything that had gone wrong with publishing in the course of his career: loud, unlettered Homer was a merchandiser pure and simple, endlessly dumping worthless tripe on the market, like the rest of the big boys, to the detriment of Literature. He cut corners, lured away authors (from Sterling in particular) with promises he had no intention of keeping, and was disrespectful of Sterling's sacrosanct authorial relationships, not to mention his vital contribution to the art of his time.

Worst of all, "I hear your boss has been sending importuning letters to Ida again," Sterling would erupt, without a shred of evidence, as Paul would discover when he pushed for it. "Does he have *any* decency? Doesn't he understand how embarrassing it is for Ida, having to turn him down year after year? Can't you do something about it, Paul?"

Sterling's misreading of Homer amused Paul, but it made him nervous, too. After all, he adored his wisecracking boss and the ramshackle enterprise he'd built, which was far more capable and dedicated to serious writing than Sterling would ever admit (the fact that he was so perennially exercised about Homer told Paul just how good Sterling knew Homer was). Besides, Homer paid Paul an unhandsome but more or less living wage, something Sterling could never have dreamed of doing.

Still, Paul couldn't quite believe how much Sterling had seen and done in his long and eccentric life in letters. Unlike Homer, who *was* essentially an organization man, however idiosyncratic, and whose first commitment was to the institution he'd so carefully created and nursed, what mattered most to Sterling was writing itself. He was a walking encyclopedia of authorial genius and malfeasance, too: the ineffable charm and unreliability of Andrei Abramovich; Marina Dello Gioio's scandalous penchant for younger men; how that so-and-so So-and-So had made it impossible for him to publish Faulkner; why his Aunt Lobelia, who'd been his major benefactor early in his career, hadn't let him publish *Lolita.* Every publisher Paul knew had a story about why someone else had prevented him from taking on the risky masterpiece that had turned out not to be risky at all. But Paul had learned over time that most publishers were haunted by the Ones That Got Away—usually thanks to their own blindness or chintziness or lack of nerve. They seemed to matter more than the ones they'd managed to snare.

As he unwound his thread during their evenings together, Sterling told Paul how he'd become a publisher at the behest of Arnold Outerbridge, when Sterling, an impetuous nineteen-year-old rich kid from Cincinnati, had decamped from the stultifying country club that was Princeton in the fall of 1946 and gone to sit at Outerbridge's feet in war-ravaged London.

Steeped in the lore and poetry of classicism, A.O. had himself been bent as a young man on remaking stolid Edwardian literature into something with the chastity of his essential Greeks. The amazing thing was that he'd done it—he and his older friends and enemies Pound, Eliot, H.D., Moore, Lawrence, and all the others. What came to be known as modernism had remade literature and the other arts once and for all. Where before you might have written, "My love is like a red, red rose" and more or less gotten away with it, suddenly there was serious talk about

> scalloped
> petals sacrificed on
> granite

(Paul looked on in amazement as Sterling threw his head back and recited Hoda Avery's "Scimitar," one of her early lyrics in her chastest imagist vein, from memory.)

Outerbridge in London, like Pound in Rapallo, had pulled the strings of his younger puppets in Oxford, New York, and San Francisco, and Sterling was among his willing captives. A.O., as Sterling needlessly reminded Paul, had been born in Nome in 1905, the son of a trapper and an Inuit woman. Somehow he got himself to Harvard, its first Alaskan student, but left after two semesters, in the spring of 1923, arguing, perhaps correctly, that the old Bostonian professorate had nothing to teach him. Instead he lit out, not for New York but London, earning his way across the Atlantic on a freighter, finding odd jobs in the metropolitan printing business, and, unbelievably, working his way deep into the beehive of English literary culture over the next decade. Ottoline Morrell took a shine to him, though Virginia Woolf found him "dull, bumptious" and T. S. Eliot studiously ignored him—until the brute force of Outerbridge's talent compelled Old Possum to acknowledge that another American was making waves in London. Pound and Eliot, older by a generation, quailed when Arnold started haranguing no one in particular about the poetic "booboisie"—a term of opprobrium stolen from his antagonist and model H. L. Mencken. Brother Arnold, as he had the temerity to call himself, lifted more than a little from Uncle Ez, though Pound affected not to notice. But on top of A.O.'s literary prowess was political commitment as well, for, like Pound, Arnold became a True Believer, though in a very different church.

When the crash came, Arnold stayed put in London, where he fell under the spell of English Communism. He went to the Spanish Civil War with John Cornford, whom he had taught during a brief stint as a master at Stowe, and was by his side when Cornford died near Córdoba the day after his twenty-first birthday, at the end of 1936. *Hesperus* (1938), A.O.'s heroic elegy for his young comrade, won him fame across the political spectrum. Suddenly, the Left had an unimpeachable literary voice, less sniffily narcissistic than Auden, more expressive and more reliably doctrinaire than Dos Passos.

The brash, contentious American had become a force to contend with in London, widely viewed as the Shelley of his age. His brief affair with Decca Mitford before her marriage to Esmond Romilly was followed by a string of conquests, most of them among the Red Debutantes of Berkeley Square. In September 1940, he married Lady Annabel Grosvenor, estranged youngest daughter of the second Duke of Westminster. Their daughter, Svetlana, was born six months later.

Outerbridge had served with courage and distinction under Montgomery in North Africa during World War II, receiving the Victoria Cross, awarded for "most conspicuous bravery or extreme devotion to duty" for his ferocity at El Alamein. His poem about Stalingrad, *Elegy for Evgenia* (Heinemann, 1946)—he and Lady Annabel had divorced quietly in 1944—became the poetic rallying cry for worldwide Communism after the war, quoted approvingly by Stalin, translated into thirty-two languages (including into Russian by the up-and-coming Yurii Khodakovsky). Sterling nonchalantly pulled the 1948 American edition off a shelf and handed it to Paul.

Awarded an honorary Red Star in 1947, A.O. was at the peak of his powers. Even the archconservative Eliot wrote (privately) that he'd been moved to tears by A.O.'s epic *The Fight* (1948; Impetus, 1949), known as the *Aeneid* of international Communism, a twenty-thousand-line narrative of Russia's devastating war the likes of which had not been seen since the days of Victor Hugo. Arnold's autobiography, *South from Nome* (1950), was likewise an international succès fou (and for decades Sterling's best-selling book. The Book-of-the-Month Club alone sold 88,000 copies the year it was published).

The Cold War, though, had been hard on A.O. From the left, the crowd around *The Protagonist* attacked his politics as retrograde and myopic, while Joe McCarthy went after him from the right. Sterling was valiant in presenting and defending Outerbridge's later work—admittedly not as strong as his heroic period—but A.O. quickly fell out of fashion in the frightened Cold War West of Eisenhower and Eden.

By the time of the Hungarian Revolution in 1956, which A.O. publicly deplored, his career in the States—and in Britain, too—was effectively over. Even in Russia, where he had been made an honorary citizen, the post-Stalinist thaw meant that Outerbridge's work went into decline under Khrushchev, and the invitations, awards, and emoluments dried up. For a while, Arnold wandered. Always writing, always it seemed with a new woman, he lived for several years on Minorca, almost within swimming distance of his old antagonist Robert Graves, and later in a remote village on the Greek island of Paros, with Svetlana, now married to a British banker, and their three boys in occasional attendance.

A.O. spent his declining years in Venice, holed up in the apartment overlooking his old flame Celine Mannheim's garden. It was there, in the fall of 1969, that he encountered Ida Perkins again (they'd had a brief affair in London in the late fifties), at a dinner for none other than Homer Stern, who was visiting his cousin. Soon Arnold and Ida were living together, and she was to care for him devotedly for the next twenty years, till he died of emphysema on October 25, 1989, at the age of eighty-four.

Sterling admitted that when he'd first come to Outerbridge in London for advice, Arnold had not been encouraging about the young Princetonian's forays into verse. "You'll never make it as a poet, Sterl," he'd drawled. "Go home and do something useful—like starting a publishing house. We need you." Crestfallen, then inspired, Sterling had spent a few months skiing and canoodling in Gstaad before wending his way home on the *Queen Mary*. Less than two years later, Impetus Editions, set up in the old farmer's cottage on his aunt Lobelia Delano's estate in Hiram's Corners, New York, a hundred miles north of the city, was a going concern.

"Impotent Editions," Outerbridge called it when he was annoyed with Sterling, which turned out to be often over the next forty years. He hadn't conceived that Sterling, beyond being loyal and well-heeled, might actually have a mind and sensibility of his own. But Impetus soon became anything but a rich man's plaything. Sterling had been tight with a dollar, he acknowledged, but liberal in his encouragement of writing that he thought mattered and the writers who created it, and over not too many years, his fledgling house had developed from a congeries of Outerbridge acolytes into a small, selective organ of the left-leaning branch of late modernism (as opposed to the by-then-incarcerated Pound's and the apotheosized Eliot's rightward-tilting brand) that came to be known as the Movement.

Paul was convinced that no one had done more to ensure the health of what became a vital alternative strain in American literature than Sterling Wainwright in his heyday. After all, Byron Hummock, the showiest of the trendsetting postwar Jewish American writers, had published his first book of stories with Sterling, as had April Owens her now-classic anti-O'Neillian dramas of modern Greek love and politics, and Jorge Metzl his groundbreaking journalism about West Africa. Sterling's Impetus New Poets also introduced and stayed loyal to most of the second- and third-generation modernists. Only Pound and his disciple Laughlin, with his comparatively staid Nude Erections, as Pound had dubbed it, established a decade earlier not thirty miles east in Connecticut's Northwest Corner, could hold a candle to the impetus that Outerbridge and Wainwright together had given to the Movement Moment.

And Sterling had evolved, too. From being a gawky, sex-obsessed, very tall rich young man, he grew into a debonair, eligible, sex-obsessed bachelor-about-town. Yes, he was something of a wastrel, along with his youthful buddy from Cincinnati Johnnie George, heir to the Skoobie Doo peanut butter fortune, who enjoyed nothing more than swanning around with Sterling and a couple of starlets for evenings on the town in New York, ski vacations in Jackson Hole, Wyoming, or trouble in Tahiti. One winter Sterling and Georgie had spent two months in the Hole, as they called it, and came away owning the ski resort at the Summit for their pains. The Summit boasted the finest powder Sterling had skied on since his student days in Switzerland, and some mighty attractive women, too. Paul had seen a picture of him making an elegant turn on a slope somewhere, a nimble industrial princeling as handsome as a matinee idol. No wonder dashing, tall, blond, rich Sterling had wowed local cattle heiress and landowner Jeannette Stevens and promptly gotten her pregnant. Jeannette was lovely and forthright in the Western way, but not all that challenging, Sterling admitted, and after giving him a daughter, she had gone back to Wyoming, baby in tow, while Sterling stayed in the East, carousing and reading and picking up writers in minuscule deals that had added up over time to a list of influence and importance, if not overwhelming salability.

By his fifties, when America was still licking its wounds over its debacle in Southeast Asia and being torn apart by the revolution in values it unleashed, the onetime playboy had evolved, Paul saw, into a literary grandee and guru, a kind of minor saint of the counterculture as the publisher and protector of his most popular author, the iconic Ida Perkins.

Sterling, as Paul didn't need reminding, had known Ida his whole life; she was his cousin, after all. Doris Appleton, the much younger half-sister of his grandmother Ida Appleton Wainwright (the Appletons hailed originally from Salem, Massachusetts, and claimed two or three witches in their lineage), had married George Peabody ("Pebo") Perkins, a stiff, Episcopalian Proper Bostonian if there ever was one, as a mere girl of eighteen in 1919; Ida's father was a hopelessly ineffectual banker who lost everything in the Crash and turned into a nasty drunk. As if that weren't enough, Pebo's brother Thomas Handyside Perkins, known as Handy, married a cousin of Sterling's mother, Lavinia Furness, so they were doubly if not exactly closely related. So Sterling and Ida were glancingly aware of each other from family gatherings throughout their childhoods, though she barely acknowledged her younger cousin's existence.

It had been at the Wainwright family's elaborate "camp"

at Otter Creek on Michigan's Upper Peninsula in 1943, the summer Sterling turned sixteen, that he'd first come alive to his older cousin's beauty. And Ida had been equally smitten with Sterling, a golf club–wielding Adonis who'd already begun turning heads, as he would all his life—Paul had heard the stories.

Sterling's infatuation with Ida, then, was not only genteelly quasi-incestuous, but had the sanctified aura of first love about it. But it wasn't simply carnal, though her flowing red locks, creamy skin, and callipygian figure were as remarkable as her aquiline profile, which today graces our 52-cent stamp. To see the cousins together was to feel you were on a movie set—except that they were so natural and unaffected, there wasn't the faintest whiff of commerce about them.

And young Ida had turned out to be a poet as well—and a supremely gifted one. No wonder Sterling, who already had the literary bug himself, fell book, line, and sinker for his beauteous lyre-strumming playmate, who at eighteen had just published her notorious first collection. Even crusty Arnold, himself more than a little dazzled by the poetic *Wundermädchen*, had dubbed her, on reading *Virgin Again* that same fateful summer, "the Sappho of Our Times."

The Sappho of Our Times was not a Sapphist, however—far from it. Her fling with her young cousin hadn't lasted long, Sterling admitted, but Paul knew it was only the first in a string of passionate liaisons destined to become the stuff of literary myth. Ida's liaisons became as legendary as Edna St. Vincent Millay's, but where Vincent had been blowzily self-advertising in her controversy-courting life and work, the young Ida was aristocratically private—ice to the outer world, a furnace within. Only H.D. and Marianne Moore approached Ida in ethereal remoteness, so dazzlingly *raffinée* next to the louche effusions of her own contemporary, the sloppy Muriel Rukeyser. No, Ida's style—cool, fragmentary, and mysterious—was entirely her own, and lent her more than a whiff of erotic glamour. "No wonder they thought she was one of the girls," Sterling joshed, downing his third single malt of the evening.

Sterling ran into the now-infamous and if anything more striking Ida in New York in the fall of 1948, and before long he was head over heels again, the way he'd been at sixteen—enough to allow him to recover at least temporarily from A.O.'s dismissal of his work and start writing again. "*Il Catullo americano*" an Italian critic had named him in his later years, the American Catullus, a moniker he wore with pride, though he could never quite muster the engorged animus that had made the Roman immortal. Sterling's love poems were generically idealizing, maybe even a little saccharine. Basically, Paul thought, he was too nice.

Ida sweeter
than upstate
Falernian
I'm waiting
here down
in the garden
under the window:
Now jump!

Not the stuff of greatness, alas. But Ida had responded. Tall, dreamy Cousin Sterling, his adolescent peachiness seasoned by a few years of romantic training, his remaining baby fat absorbed into leanness, caught her fancy again, and over that Christmas holiday they had their second torrid entanglement.

Sterling made it sound as if he'd spent a lifetime mourning those few weeks—though he'd gone on to have a rich and varied sex life of his own. He'd acquired another wife, and a son and namesake, after a series of relationships, including a long-standing, emotionally wrenching one with Bree Davis, who worked as an editor for many years at Impetus. Bree was a live wire, sensible and huskily beautiful, a kind of literary Ava Gardner, but Sterling's mother had put her foot down. He'd had one free shot; his next consort was not going to be a nobody, too. So Bree got the boot, though the *on dit* was that they'd never totally called it quits, and Sterling married Maxine Schwalbe, the self-effacing, no-nonsense, seriously wealthy daughter of the founder of Mac Labs. Sterling, who was more than a foot taller than his wife, was, Paul was aware, the less wealthy partner of the two, though Wainwright's own investments, as his protégée Bettina Braun had told Paul, brought him $10,000 a day back in the early eighties, when money was still money.

You would never have known that slight, brunette Maxine was rich, except that her effortless manners and careful democratic consideration for everyone gave her away. She didn't need to throw her not-so-considerable weight around; she needed not to. And she was loved for her selfless self, her warmth and generosity, by all who knew her, according to Bettina. Everyone but Sterling, that is. Their alliance was highly satisfactory for him, for in Maxine he finally had a good-natured mate who could create and manage a domestic establishment that catered to his every need and wish—if not desire. Desire belonged elsewhere, outside the suffocating family circle. And no doubt Maxine understood this, though she never made reference to it; that would have meant disturbing the almost courtly decorum that regulated their lives. So Maxine held firm but gentle sway in Hiram's Corners with young Sterling III, while Sterling toggled back and forth between the farm and the Impetus office he'd opened in New York in the sixties, where it was easier for him to sweet-talk wayward authors, and indulge his penchant for beautiful young things.

That was decades ago now, and a lot of water had flowed under all their bridges. Maxine had died far too young, in her late fifties, and Sterling had up and married Bree soon after. Ida was walled up in Venice with the ghost of A.O. and her showboat Italian husband. In the old days, she'd made a cross-country tour every year or two, organized by the Impetus staff, who were understandably desperate to maintain her franchise. She'd appear like royalty, magnificent in frayed velvet, silvering hair flying wild in her face, before ecstatic audiences of all ages, and then, as long as Maxine was alive at least, would drop down for a week or two of R&R at the Wainwrights' farm in Hiram's Corners, north of the city. She and Sterling had been kissing cousins, after all, and she was his best-selling author. Though their lives had long since diverged, their literary and personal ties endured. They were like family—no, they *were* family. It had been ages, though, since Ida, claiming the excuse of age, had been to America.

"The Goddess," Sterling called her more than once in the course of his evenings with Paul, with more than a hint of envy. "She barely deigns to notice us mere mortals anymore," he complained, drawing contemplatively on his amber-colored meerschaum, its bowl sculpted into a grinning satyr's head.

To which Paul had gently retorted, "Isn't she just the same as always—only older?"

"Maybe so," Sterling muttered, chewing on the stem of his pipe, then withdrawing inward, his mind already on something else, or lingering on how his and his cousin's lives had developed and diverged, tendrils from the same plant that had wound around different branches, different banisters—undeniably separate, yet still connected, still somehow one.

Paul had come upon a framed picture of them all together in Hiram's Corners on a bookshelf in Sterling's apartment, a color snapshot from the late eighties, its greens and blues leached out now. Ida, uncharacteristically wearing jeans and a straw hat, is seated between Sterling and Maxine, looking up at the photographer—most likely Sterling's daughter, Ida, her namesake. Ida P is wearing a determinedly happy smile, possibly a little careworn around the eyes. Putting a brave face on things? It was hard to tell from one photograph, one small yet precious bit of evidence, one mere tessera in the great mosaic that might fit in so many places. Who could say what those looks, those hands, those clothes, that weather truly signified? But there it was, a piece of the gone world that existed where we tread today. One sunny moment, moving inexorably toward sepia. Incredible, really, so far and yet so near: the divine Ida Perkins in Hiram's Corners, New York, holding hands with Sterling and Maxine Wainwright, smiling into the sun.

V

The Outerbridge Notebooks

One night, in Sterling's Barrow Street apartment, a floor-through in a West Village brick row house softened by elegant old Turkmen carpets, with drawings by Kandinsky and Max Ernst on the walls and a waist-high soaring Brancusi marble nude that stood voluptuously next to Sterling's chair, Paul asked about Outerbridge's last years.

"What happened to A.O. in Venice, Sterling? He seems to have gone radio silent. And what about the notebooks I understand he left behind? When are you going to publish them? When I studied his work in college, nobody even knew they existed."

Sterling was silent for a moment. "I've looked at them, but they're gobbledygook as far as I can tell," he allowed at last, in his aw-shucks staccato, meditatively sipping his sixteen-year-old Lagavulin and gazing into the embers of the fire he'd lit at the start of the evening. "They're written in code, page after page—book after book of unreadable symbols. I've never gotten around to dealing with them. Lazy, I guess. Frankly, Arnold became more or less a recluse in his later years. I'm not sure he was still all there. We pretty much fell out of touch, except through Ida."

"Could I take a look at them sometime?"

"I don't see why not," Sterling answered with a shrug. "They're in the vault at the office. Come by some afternoon."

The Impetus offices, in a venerable Meatpacking District building not far from Sterling's apartment, were at least as scruffy as P & S's, with upholstery that looked lice-infested and filthy walls that had not been washed, let alone painted, in forty years. Still, they commanded a panoramic view of the harbor, including the Statue of Liberty, Staten Island, and the Verrazano Bridge, from the terrace that girded them. The old bank vault was in the business office at the end of the hall, which was lined with familiar photos of some of Sterling's principal authors, including a beetling, rather intimidating one of A.O. and, farther on, a wispy, out-of-focus Ida in a style reminiscent of Virginia Woolf's great-aunt Julia Margaret Cameron.

Sterling spun the dial, swung open the safe's heavy army-green door, and rifled through a rat's nest of manuscripts and ledgers, finally producing an old grocery box from the bottom shelf. The notebooks were piled inside, Venetian laid paper edged with gold bound in grained red leather. There were thirteen of them, each ninety-six pages, about nine by eleven inches. Every surface was covered with writing—numbers, letters, and symbols in ordered rows, page after page of them, all in uniform red ink. At the bottom of the box was a large accordion file stuffed with crumbling newspaper clippings, articles, and other ephemera.

Clearly, Outerbridge had had something to say in his last years in Venice, but he hadn't wanted anyone to know what it was, at least not anytime soon. Paul was intrigued. He asked Sterling if he could look the notebooks over more thoroughly.

"Be my guest," Sterling conceded amiably. "Maybe we'll both learn something."

Paul made several visits to Impetus to pore over the notebooks after work. He got to know the staff—those he hadn't already met in his years in the business, that is. They struck him as a clannish bunch, suspicious of the corrupted world outside the Impetus walls. He felt a solidarity with them he wasn't sure was fully shared, given that he worked for one of Sterling's longtime nemeses in Commercial Publishing. Still, they too were lifers, not all that different from the inmates on Union Square, and he hoped he'd eventually be accepted as part of the family—a loud, clueless distant relation, maybe, visiting interminably from Elsewhere.

The notebooks themselves, though, made no sense at all. In form they resembled poems, but they were written in what looked like an abstruse computer language:

&/x#xewhh

hd/zxk66cc
wde9x+#}#>3$a#
ezd/zx3$.+a#>>k++a
eed%hx2$#.x+k$c>)c++a
e%df9x6;k$a
e9d/zxvk4c—+;k>=x+;>wv

Sometimes, the “poems” were interrupted by series of longer lines:

;!vc#}#+xvc#}^x4c3ac}#+x@c}^x$c|$ac}#+
$k#31#^x+k+3c>$k3xaw#@kyx6k$cvc#3x6kk|2|c!2

At first Paul was totally stymied by the impenetrability of A.O.’s gobbledygook, but as he hunkered down, he could see patterns emerge. He asked if he could borrow the notebooks, but Sterling demurred: “They don’t belong to me; they’re Svetlana’s”—Arnold’s daughter, who lived in London. “I’d be responsible if anything happened to them.”

So whenever he could steal time from his regular duties, Paul worked alone late into the evening, bent over the old metal desk in the fluorescent-lit back office, laboriously mapping the notebooks, trying to identify recurrences in Arnold’s symbols. At times the work was so stultifying that he felt like giving up. But he wanted to impress Sterling with his industry and ingenuity, so he kept at it, searching doggedly for some way into their mystery.

Then one evening, out of the blue, after one of their whiskey-lubricated confabs had stretched long into the wee hours, the old man made Paul an unexpected offer.

"Why don't you come spend your vacation up in Hiram's Corners? You can keep chipping away at these cussed things, and we can keep talking about Arnold and Ida and everything else."

It was more than a dream come true; it was the fulfillment of a dream Paul hadn't known he'd had. He didn't fully understand why he was so drawn to Sterling, as he was in a different way to Homer, these figures from another era, these competing fathers. As someone who'd always felt faintly fatherless himself and who was always quietly searching for mentors, he found that each loomed in his psyche in his own unsettling way. Homer, outlandish, imposing, larger than life, was the immutable sun around which everything in his universe revolved. Sterling was cooler; he had the nonchalance, the charm and modesty and arrogance, of the privileged man nothing had ever stood in the way of. He was tall, though at his age his knees gave slightly when he walked, so he had no doubt been even more imposing as a beautiful young man. Now he ambled along like a daddy longlegs with or without cane, still slim and elegant, still sure he was the handsomest man in the room, yet innocent of the self-love that emanated from Homer like a musk.

Paul understood that Homer and Sterling represented worldly effectiveness, a congruity of aspiration and achievement that Paul wanted for himself. The trouble was, they hated each other. Paul felt tarred by Homer's brush when he was with Sterling, and vice versa: too venal for Impetus-like sainthood, too airy-fairy literary for a he-man's world of fucking and cigars. When he was with one or the other, Paul made light of their antipathy, as they themselves did, to their credit, yet he had an uneasy intuition—or was it simply a projection?—that each man wanted him all to himself. Each commanded his loyalty. Homer was Paul's chief enabler, the senior partner in the rough-and-tumble game they both enjoyed so much, often precisely because of its (relatively civilized, to be sure) rugby scrum–like mixing it up. But Paul esteemed and aspired to emulate Sterling's taste and finesse, too. Now here he was, employed by Homer but moonlighting on a project for Sterling. It was an uncomfortable place to be, like so many others he'd found himself in.

Much the same was true, in a different way, of his relationship with Jasper Bewick, the fetching young music critic he'd been pining over for the past couple of years, ever since his on-again, off-again thing with Tony Heller had come to an end. Tony was an actor who filled in as a waiter at the Crab, and he'd played the part of a boyfriend beautifully, until their run was suddenly over. There'd been a long period of misunderstandings and hurt feelings and what felt like betrayals, until they both had the sense to end it. After Tony's aimlessness, Jasper's rash enthusiasms and 24/7 seductiveness, not to mention his wavy dark hair and compact, muscular body, had been catnip for Paul—as had Jasper's push-me-pull-you, *fort/da* ambivalence. Jasper clearly needed Paul around. The trouble was he didn't seem to *want* Paul, least of all as a lover. They would have long, intense dinners during which they'd talk about music, literature, their families, Jasper's dreams of fame—everything under the sun—but when Paul walked him to his doorway, Jasper would give him a brotherly hug and disappear upstairs.

When Paul pulled away, though, Jasper was there in a flash—with unobtainable concert tickets, premium-grade gossip, and pouty protestations of need and affection. This had been going on long enough for Paul to recognize, in his moments of lucidity, that he and Jasper had no future. But he was a sucker for Jasper's beauty and brilliance and charm—which meant he was stuck with their stuckness, treading water, as he always did when it came to romance. It depressed him to think about it, so he tried to concentrate on his work, and on the notebooks, though they seemed as impossible to find his way into as Jasper's arms.

When August first rolled around, Paul invited Jasper to drive up for a visit, using the local music festival as bait, though he had little expectation he would bite. Paul bid Homer and his office mates a fond farewell and headed for Hiram's Corners in his rented red Hyundai with his heart in his mouth. He felt a little bit like a character in a Grimm's fairy tale, disappearing into the fragrant forest with no trail of crumbs to help him to find his way home.

VI

Lost in Hiram's Corners

High in the foothills of the Middlesex Mountains, Hiram's Corners was far enough from New York City to be a world unto itself, not the weekenders' outpost that towns across the Connecticut border like Kent or Salisbury had become—enclaves of rich urbanites who owned most of the notable property in town and kept the locals employed maintaining it. Hiram's Corners differed from other wealthy suburban watering holes in that its grandees were homegrown. It sometimes seemed that all the large landholders in the town were related. The Wainwrights' presence went back to Sterling's great-aunt Aurelia, a big-bosomed Cincinnati matron with a lorgnette and sensible shoes who had married her way east when she was younger and lither. Adelbert Binns, whom she'd wed in 1905, had made good as John D. Rockefeller's chief fixer at Standard Oil and had been handsomely rewarded in the process. Binns belonged to another notable Cincinnati tribe; he'd put down roots here on the advice of old Senator Hiram Handspring, who had likewise married into the family. Over the years his son Bobby Binns, and Bobby's son Beebe, a noted conservationist, nationally recognized orchid grower, and devotee of the Middlesex woods, had acquired more than eight thousand acres on the slopes of Bald Mountain, reputedly one of the largest private holdings in the state outside the Adirondacks. The Wainwrights' mere several hundred acres hugged the edge of this spread and were effectively part of it.

The Binnses over time had created a Currier and Ives world of rambling old houses, orchards, and rolling fields amid the pond-studded woodland of Hiram's Corners. Other relations of Aurelia's had followed her here—including her niece Lobelia Wainwright Delano, Sterling's aunt, until the whole east side of Hiram's Corners facing the Middlesex Mountains, which rose gently a few miles beyond, was one large swath of Binns/Delano/Wainwright lands. Ida and Sterling, though they had fallen for each other in Michigan, had spent winter holidays here, too, at extended-family house parties, engaging, or not engaging, in the activities—snowshoeing and cross-country skiing by day; skating by the light of the bonfires built on the ice of Handspring Pond, playing bridge, and drinking by night—that made up life in the Magic Kingdom.

There was something about the changeless tranquillity of the place—the large, unfarmed farms with their well-tended meadows and woods; the lack of change in their ownership; the deep, deep cold of the long, long winters. When Sterling's Aunt Lobelia had settled here in the twenties, she'd built herself a Palladian mansion on a rock ledge on River Road. After Sterling had come to his senses and returned from London, she'd constructed a tall, boxy wooden house for him across the street, and let him set up Impetus Editions in the farmer's house beyond the meadow. In between the Cow Cottage, as it was known, and his aunt were nothing but birch and maple fern woods scattered with towering rhododendrons and flame azaleas that blazed bright orange in June.

On Paul's first evening, he walked down the grassy old woods road that ran past the cottage like something out of a poem by Robert Frost. It wound over a rickety bridge, up a steep hill, and across a pine forest plateau, then descended beside a swamp that was home to Venus flytrap and other carnivorous plants, passing a small, unoccupied screen-porched cottage on the right. After another slight incline it arrived at Handspring Pond and Aunt Lobelia's stone "camp," a Beaux Arts gem in its own right, with Sterling's shingled one a few hundred feet to the east. Sprinkled around the edge of the little lake were a dozen similar structures, most of them owned by the several branches of the Binns family. The only noise that intruded on the pond, where motorboats were forbidden, was an occasional shout from the beach at the west end, which Beebe leased to the town for a dollar a year. The woods roads and trails in the Bald Mountain Forest passed many wonders—secret lakes, cellars of settlements abandoned centuries ago, even occasional patches of primeval first-growth forest, the ultimate rarity.

The photos of Hiram's Corners in the mid-nineteenth century that Paul saw at the Historical Society on the town green were shocking: these densely green hills had, like most of the Eastern Seaboard, been virtually shorn of forest by charcoalers avid to feed the kilns of the small iron factories that lined the Huckleberry River, which was little more than a big brook, before the invention of steel. The very innovations that had been the sources of the Wainwrights' and Binnses' wealth—oil, coal, and steel—had killed off these little enterprises and tens of thousands like them and allowed those brash nineteenth-century Midwestern arrivistes to become the lords of Hiram's Corners. And now oil and steel had been shoved aside by what—high tech? Everyone was waiting for the first dot-commers to show up in Middlesex. So far, though, it seemed to have been passed over by the new Masters of the Universe in favor of showier spots. Being up in the hills, Hiram's Corners didn't even have high-speed Internet access, a bone of contention, Paul soon learned, for the few transplanted New Yorkers who wanted to live and work here. It was a place out of time, nearly feudal in its hierarchies and peaceableness. Paul lay back in his chaise longue and breathed in its self-satisfied woodsy air like perfume.

The Cow Cottage had originally been built as the farmer's house on Aunt Lobelia's property. Like her own aunt Aurelia, she'd arrived from Cincinnati, one of those reverse pioneers who made their way back to the original Colonies to acquire the patina of gentility that was missing in the Western Reserve. Aunt Lobelia was stolid and a little self-righteous, but devoted to her brother's wayward yet alert only son, and indulgent, up to a point, of his odd interest in the arts. When Sterling had decided to become a publisher, she'd created a sylvan refuge in which he could pursue his literary aspirations away from the intermittently prying eyes of his intermittently disapproving parents and under her conventional but benevolent nose.

A succession of writers had lived in the Cottage, helping Sterling conduct Impetus business and holding down the fort when he took off for the Summit, where he still spent much of every winter, skiing, snowshoeing, and transforming the place into a Spartan but first-world-class ski resort, and visiting Jeannette and their daughter, Ida, named, he said, for his Wainwright grandmother.

In his absence, first Harold Cowden, then Konrad Preuss, and lastly Eli Mandel, all of them among Sterling's second string of indigent young writers, had tried to make a go of working for subsistence wages in the upper Hudson Valley with no one to see or talk to except the naturally curious—i.e., suspicious—locals, who didn't know a villanelle from a bottle of bourbon. Cowden had got a book out of it—his *Hiram's Corners Cantata*, usually viewed as an aberration in his work—before being briefly institutionalized. Preuss and Mandel, perhaps better balanced, had lasted less long. Then Sterling established the Impetus New York office and bought the Barrow Street apartment (useful for authorial conferences that sometimes turned into trysts and/or vice versa), and the work and play of Impetus Editions had largely moved south. But to the initiated, the Cow Cottage retained its aura of literary sanctity, and the attached barn, with its mullioned Swiss windows, was stocked with Sterling's overflow library of IE books, a veritable temple to the literary cult he'd established. It was here that Paul had set up shop to work on A.O.'s notebooks.

Paul shared Sterling's view that A.O. was the only Red poet who had not been bested by ideology. As with his model Shelley, Arnold's superabundant lyric gift surpassed and, some would say, annihilated the ideas he expressed, till all there was, in effect, was the poetry—its thrust and lilt steamrolling the poet's purported convictions. Paul could practically taste the romance of A.O.'s life in Venice with Ida, she consoling him about the eternal vagaries of politics and reminding him of the enduring power of his voice, Arnold urging her on to ever-new delvings, new castles in Spain, new amazements to be pulled out of the humid Venetian breeze, composing his mysterious encrypted poems all the while.

But this wasn't Venice. Paul was here in this idyllic yet unfamiliar place, with a daunting task in front of him. He'd taken up the study of ciphers, having ordered every guide he could find on the Medusa website that didn't sound too technical. He felt guilty about patronizing the rapacious online bookseller, but the truth was that Styx and Stonze never had what he needed, even in their Madison Square flagship store, where board games and wrapping paper and the book chain's own proprietary product were beginning to squeeze out books. What would Morgan think? he wondered—a bit disingenuously, since he already knew.

Paul had convinced himself that it was just a matter of time before he'd find the method in A.O.'s madness. Working in the airless barn wasn't always conducive to code-cracking, though. Some days, he'd spend more time than he'd have liked to admit *not* working on the notebooks, fretting about the non-life he was leading or poring over Sterling's secondary—or was it tertiary?—library of Impetus titles, alphabetically arranged on unpainted shelves with old juice bottles for bookends. Everyone from Tagore to Blaisdell, early Luteri to late Broch, Robert Duncan to Dermott Weems to César Vallejo to Pélieu to Serenghetti—it was a checkerboard of world literature, mind-boggling in its breadth and adventurousness and originality. Yes, Sterling liked to talk about the ones that got away but, my God, the ones he'd landed, the cavalcade of writers he'd discovered, nurtured, and kept in print over a long and no doubt often discouraging but ultimately triumphant career!

The truth was that many of these names, the makers of modern culture, had sold very little over the course of their long lives in print with Impetus. It was one of the realities of publishing: what was truly new often languished in the warehouse nearly unasked-for. One of the tricks of publishing was catching the wave of public taste at the right moment. If you were too prescient, too far ahead of the swell, literally nothing would happen—until lightning struck, if it did, years, sometimes decades, later. In the meantime, you had to have other ways of keeping body and soul together to be a serious writer—or a publisher. The remarkable thing about Sterling was how he'd used his means, and used them brilliantly, to build his house. With Aunt Lobelia's help, he'd husbanded his modest stake and kept his shoestring operation going long enough, consistently enough, devotedly enough, that fifty years on he had a catalog that was the envy of the more discerning of his commercial confreres. And Impetus had eventually become profitable as well, when a goodly number of its key authors had ended up being adopted in classrooms across America. The long tail had paid off for Sterling. Not that this was why he'd done it;

but commercial success in the end was heroic confirmation of the essential soundness of his undertaking. He'd made a wager with fate that out of desire, stick-to-itiveness, and judgment, he could create a worthwhile publishing venture. And he'd succeeded; by trusting his own taste, he'd shown them all—his uncomprehending family, his derisive competitors, even crusty, superior Arnold Outerbridge, who'd taken a left-handed chance on a brash young layabout.

Paul hadn't come into publishing at a time when with a little money and a lot of taste and elbow grease you could build something like an Impetus or a P & S. Besides, he didn't have the cash or the chutzpah to start something on his own. By the time he'd shown up, most of the smaller houses had been gobbled up by so-called general-interest publishers, most of them now owned in turn by much bigger conglomerates who'd publish anything they could get their hands on that had a chance of making money, and whose lists consequently more or less resembled one another. Impetus and P & S were anomalies now, among the last of the independents, whose lists reflected the tastes and commitments of the publishers themselves. It was unclear how long they'd hold out in the rush for consolidation and "scale" that was whipping through the book business and countless others like a tornado through a hay field.

Still, Paul hoped that in his work with Homer he could

emulate the single-mindedness and finesse that Sterling had brought to realizing his dream. Paul believed in believers—not the credulous religious, but those who aspired to move the needle, to add something to the world. What he valued most was their all-or-nothing faith in themselves—something he wished he had more of—accompanied by the self-forgetting that true love requires. Aspiration to him didn't feel like self-seeking.

So he daydreamed a lot in that often stifling back room, with dead flies in the cobwebs and the dust of slowly disintegrating books in the air—and not always about the shambles of his love life. He was taken with the hodgepodge of images tacked on the beams: an early Impetus logo by Alfonso Ossorio (which he later convinced Sterling to frame and hang in the house); an ink sketch of A.O. in his most prophetic mode; a dog-eared eighteenth-century print of the Forum; that eye-opening photo of Sterling moguling on the Swiss slopes; a peeling, blunt-cornered postcard of Celine Mannheim's half-finished Venetian palazzo; a snapshot of Ida dancing the frug with Robert Duncan in a San Francisco gay bar.

He could hear bees out in the garden, under the gigantic, unthreatening clouds. He could see the hollyhocks and roses distorted by the bottle-green glass of the barn windows. He didn't know which was more attractive: the sun-drenched world outside the barn; the barn itself with its beckoning treasures; or the pages on the desk in front of him, the paper trail, the leavings of the man who had written more than a few of the classic books arrayed around him. Part of him wanted to be outside in the cool air, so clean it hurt his citified lungs, weeding the lily beds or editing the woods, as Sterling had joked when he'd come upon him one day, piling up brush in the thin stand of birches behind the house for exercise. But he wanted to be here inside, too, with the ephemera of his heroes' lives. He didn't know how to choose, so he sat doing nothing, till he felt the chill of a sudden storm through the door he'd left open.

Reluctantly, he rose and went to make sure the windows were shut in the cottage. The rain raged, and the power went out for an hour. After a while, his laptop's battery died, so he flipped through the papers in the accordion file, inhaling the smoky residue of Arnold's and Ida's lives. The charred smell came, he assumed, from the pages themselves, burning away invisibly as they had for years in the Impetus vault in New York. Eventually they would crumble and be lost to the world, if they weren't thrown away first. For today, though, they were his to inhale and get lost in. Utter joy, joy he knew no one else could understand or share in, joy like a secret perversion possessed him, and in those moments in the barn Paul was guiltily, radiantly happy, wallowing in his heroes' lives as if they were his own.

* * *

Late in the day he usually strolled down to the dock to join Sterling and Bree for a swim. It was like clockwork: at four o'clock the old station wagon would trundle past the Cow Cottage and Paul would know Sterling would be spending the next hour or two down at the pond, occasionally dipping in the water but mainly sunning and gabbing with Bree and Ida and his son-in-law Charlie Bernstein and their kids and whoever else happened to be around.

Next door to Sterling's was the camp of Seamus O'Sullivan, a jerry-built wooden affair with a proliferation of porches, balconies, and docks from which many-colored bath towels were perpetually waving like banners in the breeze. Seamus, a longtime staff writer at *The Gothamite*, where he had been both the jazz and the racing critic for decades, considered himself a bon vivant and a wit. He also fancied himself a bosom buddy of Sterling's, and he was constantly seeking to engage him in barbed banter studded with classical taglines from their school days. But Paul thought he could detect a certain detachment in Sterling's repartee, and a corresponding neediness underneath Seamus's affectionate raillery. Paul had begun to understand that Sterling was always just a little bit absent with everyone. He let things happen, he played along, but there was a plane of his attention that seemed unreachable.

Today, as it happened, it was just Bree on the dock with Sterling. She was knitting, chuckling as Sterling commented on the news and made derisive noises about the Higher Social Orders over at Serenity Lake, the other body of water in Hiram's Corners, whom the Handspring Pond denizens enjoyed condescending to. There wasn't much of a breeze this afternoon, and the one Sunfish out on the pond, manned by Rick Binns with a new blond passenger, wasn't making much headway.

Paul, his head full of his work in the barn, asked Sterling about Outerbridge's visit to Hiram's Corners with Ida. "When were they here?"

"Must have been in seventy-nine, when A.O. got his honorary degree from Harvard—an honorary A.B., in fact; as you know, he never graduated.

"It was quite an afternoon," Sterling continued. "A.O. wasn't talking. It was in his period of Silent Protest against the way he'd been treated in the McCarthy years. But Ida was wonderful. She made the whole thing as natural as an ice-cream social with her nonstop chatter, while attending to Arnold's every need."

Paul noticed that Bree had stopped knitting and was looking out over the pond, at what he couldn't tell.

"How old was she then?"

"Let's see. A.O. was seventy-four, so she would have been in her early fifties. But she looked much younger. She always has. Her flawless skin, her carriage, her piercing green eyes—she's always been twenty years younger than her actuarial age. And acted it, too! No, there's no one like Ida. Never was, never will be."

Paul hadn't heard Sterling talk this way before. He was being sentimental! Paul had read enough of the man's poetry to know the many varieties of amorousness he could affect, most of them patent hot air, and probably meant to be taken as such. But there was a kind of straight-up idealization in his reminiscing today that was unlike him, in Paul's admittedly limited experience.

"What did she talk about?"

"Everything and nothing, like any normal person. She made wonderful conversation, kept things going as if there were nothing unusual or untoward about Arnold's behavior. She covered for him. You would never have known that, of the two of them, she was arguably the greater writer. By a country mile."

Bree was rising now, stuffing her knitting into her bag. "It's time to be going, Sterling," she said, though it was only five, unusually early for them to be leaving the dock.

"Read her, my boy," Sterling advised Paul, as he struggled to his feet. "Read her."

"Oh, I've read her, Sterling," he answered. "I think I know her almost by heart."

"Just checking," Sterling snorted. "She's the one, you know, boy. She's the one." Then he followed Bree up the steps, and in a minute Paul heard the station wagon turning over and slowly trundling up the woods road.

He spent the evening immersed in Ida yet again—there were multiple copies of all her books in the barn. As always, he tried to feel his way into her life through her poems, but there was something elusive, indistinct, about the objects or catalysts of her own precisely evoked feelings, though Paul knew her amorous itinerary inside out. But he was beginning to hear Ida differently in her poems than he had before. True, her love objects were all gorgeous antagonists, virtually interchangeable conquered conquerors shorn of their manhood along with their locks, as in the infamous "Verga" of 1943, written when she was just eighteen:

sleep while you can while
the sun is still roaming
white body tarred
by its cyclamen stain

night-haired Endymion
splayed in the gloaming
stay in my arms
till its coming again

Yet as Ida aged, as life flowed through her veins, Paul began to detect a subtle change in her explorations of eros. It was as if gradually she became able to entertain feelings of vulnerability and insufficiency. And her portrayals of self then could be heartrending:

> Look for me under my pinafore
> under your skin
> reckless and shivering
> ravenous wild-
> eyed and thin

Ida's work developed, and changed, too, as she aged. And at times her heroic self-sufficiency began to feel like simple sadness.

* * *

The next morning, it was back to work in the barn. After a long slog, he felt he was beginning to make headway. Slowly, by a grim, steadfast process of elimination, he'd begun to break into Arnold's code.

He'd started with some long lines, predominately in the later notebooks, which were repetitions in every possible permutation and in numberless styles of penmanship, upper- and lowercase, of just three symbols: A, 3, and #.

AAAAAAAAAAAAAAAAAAAAAAAAAAAAAAAAAAA
3333333333333333333333333333333333333333333333
##

or sometimes

##
aaaaaaaaaaaaaaaaaaaaaaaaaaaaaaaaaaaaaaaaaaaaaaaaaaaa
3333333333333333333333333333333333333333333333

or

3333333333333333333333333333333333333333333333
##
AAAaaaAAaaAaAaAaAaAaAaaaaaAAAAAAaAaaAAaaAAaA

Paul decided to adopt the hypothesis that these frequently repeated figures represented the letters of Ida's name, which often appeared uncoded, too—row after row of *I*'s and *D*'s and *A*'s—in the last notebooks. After that, a statistical matchup of the most common letter frequencies—he remembered good old *etaoin shrdlu* on the Linotype—started to produce results. Words began to form out of the blind symbology of A.O.'s lines, like figures emerging from the mist. The frequency tables needed some adjustment, though, because many of the words—again, unsurprisingly—were Italian, in which the most commonly used letters are *eaoin lrtsc*.

A.O.'s method turned out to be fairly straightforward, and Paul realized to his dismay that if he'd bothered to consult an expert he could have deciphered the notebooks long ago. Arnold's encoding wasn't quite as primitive as a Caesar's cipher, where one letter substitutes for another a set number of places down the alphabet. Instead, he had replaced the letters and numbers with an arbitrary list of symbols: # for *a*, © for *b*, ¥ for *c*, *x* for a letter space, *d* for a colon. Certain letters and numbers stood in for others: *a* for *i*, and 3 for *d*, *k* for *o*, *g* for 6, for instance, which it took Paul several long sessions to figure out. Paul's hypothesis had been correct: when Arnold meant IDA, he'd written A3#.

Once he'd deciphered them, though, the notebooks hadn't, unfortunately, proven to be all that edifying. The "poems" turned out to be accountings of everything A.O. had done, day in and day out, hour by hour, sometimes minute by minute, in Venice:

23 APRIL 1986

8:30 coffee
9:15 lavanderia
10:36 Dr. Giannotti
11:28 Sra. Lorenzetti
12:45 fuori

15:30 home—long lunch
16:29 Sterling call
18:40 bath
19:30 Moro cocktails
21:00 dinner
22:59 bed—red room

24 APRIL 1986

8:29 caffè, cornetto
9:09 shoemaker
11:19 plumber
14:30 Giannotti . . .

The entries went on inexorably this way, covering roughly the last five years of A.O.'s life—before dementia seemed to leave him entirely incoherent, that is, though his daily jottings had continued even then. In the last notebook the scribbling became wilder, less concise and organized. The diary entries ceased and all that was left were chains of words, which could go on for pages:

upheaval heavy medieval bevy retrieval seawall scorch

levee steady level conundrum grief set piece

Muse

alstroemeria astronomy aphid Arthurian unstable unspeakable

table unable

roadway goldenrod icebox forehead footsteps possess embrace

No poems, no revelations or confessions. Just lists of appointments interspersed with strings of seemingly random words. And Ida's name, in various permutations, in and out of code, repeated over and over.

Arnold's notebooks remained opaque. Whatever meaning they held was locked inside them, maybe forever. Paul had succeeded in unscrambling their code, perhaps—or were these supposed diary entries a cipher of their own, with yet another layer of secrets beneath them? Their writer's deeper imperative, the one that had determined the words on the pages, remained unfathomed.

Paul had been working his way through the old accordion file he'd found with the notebooks, too. It wasn't just clippings, it turned out, but carbons of correspondence to and from Impetus and others concerning both A.O. and Ida—bills, letters from Sterling to both of them, along with some answers from Arnold—though, of course, nothing from her. Reading them was like watching Ida's fame balloon.

It was the publication of *Bringing Up the Rear* in 1954 that had signaled her emergence from the chrysalis of cultdom into public fame. Even the aging Wallace Stevens had written Sterling to say, "She gives me hope for our future." Her kinsman Robert Lowell, only eight years Ida's senior, who'd also had a stellar career early on, winning the Pulitzer Prize when he was barely thirty, had watched her speed by him like a literary Road Runner. Still, he couldn't help but praise the "brilliance, finish, and freedom" of Ida's work in his *Sewanee Review* review of *Bringing Up the Rear.* Ida was a Brahmin, too, every bit as much as Cal; but she had none of the self-protective entitlement he'd had to work so assiduously to shed; it just slid off her back like rainwater. Lowell could only look on in stunned confusion.

Then there was a July 23, 1960, letter to Sterling from the manager of the Chelsea Hotel, enclosing a bill for almost $12,000:

> *Miss Ida Perkins and her coterie left hurriedly this morning after more than a month here at the Chelsea without settling their account. As she provided your name in case of emergencies, I am sending it on to you for satisfaction.*

Or this one, from Sterling to A.O., dated February 28, 1970:

> *Dearest Arnold:*
>
> *My spies tell me the powder at the Summit is peerless this season, but I haven't been able to get away, largely due*

to the run on Ida's work. We've reprinted Half a Heart *thirteen times since the National Book Award, and my salesmen tell me the stores can't keep it on the shelves. And* all *of her work is going gangbusters. E. S. Wilentz collared me in front of his shop on Eighth Street this morning and wouldn't stop chanting, "SEND. ME. MORE. BOOKS." It was embarrassing—and sublime. Of course we don't* have *books to send him at the moment, but the printer promised another twenty thousand next week. Twenty thousand! Our cynical old sales manager Sidney Huntoon says it'll be "Gone today, here tomorrow," once the excitement dies down, but in Ida's case, I don't think so for once. The old girl is the absolute toast of the town. You should have seen her on* Dick Cavett, *making eyes and getting him to laugh uproariously. And her show with Audrey Dienstfrey and Her Kind was a sellout at Boston Garden. Audrey screamed and wept and made an enormous scene—envious, no doubt—but now they're joined at the hip and Audrey won't let her new soul sister out of her sight.*

You'd be proud of your consort. I certainly am. We're minting money, for once. Ida seems to be enjoying it all—at least most of it; I don't think she's wild about being mobbed in the street. Luckily, she's coming up to the farm for the weekend to hide out, bringing that ingrate Hummock and maybe young John Ashbery along. Yawn. Maxine has orga-

nized a little golf tourney for everyone that ought to be a riot, since most of the guests aren't exactly star athletes.

In other news, I'm sorry to report that we're going to have to let Elegy for Evgenia *go out of stock for the time being, as demand has fallen below the acceptable threshold for a reprint. Here's hoping the situation turns around shortly.*

I trust all is otherwise serene in La Serenissima. Keep the faith; we're holding on as usual here.

Ever thine,

There were ecstatic reviews and the inevitable pans, particularly of *Barricade* and *The Brownouts*, published in Ida's so-called Anti phase. There were endless award citations: four National Book Awards (and a photograph of Ida arm in arm with fellow winners Joyce Carol Oates and William Steig at the awards dinner in 1992); two Pulitzer Prizes; the Feltrinelli, Lenin, Nonino, Prince of Asturias, Jerusalem, and T. S. Eliot prizes; the gold medal for poetry of the American Academy of Arts and Letters; a letter from 41 offering Ida the Presidential Medal of Freedom (with a carbon of a reply from Sterling politely declining on her behalf); a list of thirty-nine honorary degrees, from 1960 to 2005; copies of full-page advertisements for various titles; articles in *Flair* and *Vogue* about her idiosyncratic fashion sense; bills from Bergdorf Goodman for thousands of dollars, primarily for shoes; travel agents' invoices from the triumphal 1967 West Coast tour, during which Ida had cavorted naked in the big pool at Esalen with Pepita Erskine, after spending the weekend in Watts with Eldridge Cleaver. A photo of sunburned, shirtless Allen Ginsberg and Robert Lowell flanking a pale, straw-hatted Ida, taken by Elizabeth Hardwick on Mount Desert Island in August 1968, two days after the *New York Post* printed the iconic shot of Ida in a Chanel suit with matching spectator pumps and alligator bag outside La Côte Basque with Babe Paley and Truman Capote ("Whose Hair Higher?" the caption queried). Invitations to twelve state dinners at the White House, from the Johnson to Obama administrations. A royalty statement for *Aria di Giudecca* (7,238 copies sold in the first six months of 2000).

And there was this, from 1964:

Dear Mr. Wainwright:

I want to thank you for sending Ida Perkins's new book, The Face-lift Wars, *which I have been nibbling at with great fascination since its arrival. Miss Perkins is that unlikely miracle, a Real Thing. Gertrude Stein, who as you know encouraged Ida when she was still a girl, would have been gratified to see how she has panned out.*

With appreciation,
Alice Toklas

* * *

That night Paul had troubled dreams, of Ida and Sterling and A.O. and Gertrude Stein and Mao and Gloria Steinem (and Jasper, too) caught in bizarre conflicting situations, battles, triangles, thrashing sex, and misery—and him on the sidelines, not knowing how to enter in, to engage or calm them. He woke headachy and exhausted, and spent another rainy day in the barn finishing up his transcription, which that day seemed boring and pointless. He was sick of them all, and most of all sick of himself and his voyeuristic need to live through them. Luckily, it would soon be time to pack up and head back to the city.

First, though, Homer was coming for a visit. He'd called to announce that he and Iphigene were driving up to Hiram's Corners to check in on Paul—"consorting with the enemy," he'd put it good-humoredly enough, though he'd been disparaging about Outerbridge when Paul had admitted he was working with Sterling on the notebooks. Maybe Homer was curious about how his old competitor lived; his own country place was a turn-of-the-century Tyrolean chalet in Westchester originally built by his great-uncle that now, unfortunately, backed onto the Saw Mill River Parkway. Or maybe it was simple boredom that sent him out of the house. In any case, Paul decided to invite Sterling and Bree to lunch at the Cow Cottage on the Sterns' visiting day. He fixed a shrimp salad, iced tea, and icebox cookies, and waited for the fireworks.

It had gone well, much to his relief. Sterling presented Homer with a rare copy of a Hiram's Corners Chapbook of Elspeth Adams's *First Poems*, and Homer had been visibly touched. They'd all chatted cordially about the weather, their children, and various authors, steering clear, for the most part, of the ones they'd "shared" (i.e., fought over) and moving on to the general decline of the business and the perfidy of agents—subjects the two old lions were in utter agreement about. And then, after a couple of hours of making nice, Homer and Iphigene had been on their way. Ida had gone unmentioned, needless to say—after all, there were other ladies at the table—but in Paul's mind, and who knows, perhaps in the other men's, too, she had been vividly present.

He'd imagined her suddenly appearing: lunch on Olympus, *le déjeuner sur l'herbe*, all of them immortally young, feasting nude on nectar and ambrosia. Instead, it had been a congenial little meal, a moment of truce between aged warriors—with nothing to arouse their old rivalry.

"He's mellowed," Homer said about Sterling when Paul was back at work—which was precisely what Sterling had told Paul down at the dock that afternoon. The good feeling lasted a few weeks, and then they were back to what they enjoyed most: doing each other down to Paul. He was caught in the middle, as usual. Yet he felt abler now to move back and forth between his heroes. He'd been with both of them at the same time and place and no one had even raised his voice.

VII

Sunny Days at P & S

"How was your weekend, dearie? Read anything interesting?"

Paul, who'd been back at work for a few weeks, was sitting in Homer's corner office with him and Sally, as they did most mornings after she'd taken Homer's dictation. The company's ratty style extended to the boss's inner sanctum, which, though larger than the other offices and furnished with a conference table and a dirt-encrusted Danish modern desk and two sweat-stained aquamarine leather armchairs, was every bit as shabby as the rest of the premises. The cracked linoleum floor was waxed fairly often, filth and all, so it was shiny as well as grubby. Thirty-year-old curtains of a beige indistinguishable from dinge framed windows overlooking Union Square, which was currently experiencing a renaissance that had made it the teenage hangout capital of Manhattan. Now, instead of users scoring at the foot of the Civil War monument in the center of the park, recovering users competed with after-schoolers, dog walkers, and the occasional hardy passerby for seats on the too-few benches. Still, the greenmarket that happened four days a week right outside the office was a boon. Paul occasionally saw Homer and Sally shopping for fruit or flowers on their daily post-prandial stroll.

"Not much. A few no-count novels."

"When is that momser Burns going to finish his book? He owes us a small fortune. If he'd lay off shtupping that girl of his with the ring in her nose and get down to work, we'd all be a lot better off."

"That's a bindi Anjali wears on her forehead, Homer. Earl phoned last week to say he's about to deliver."

Homer's banter with Paul kept things lively and safely impersonal between them. His constant stream of gossip, especially the sexual variety, invariably contained juicy tid-bits about whoever was current on his ever-active shit list. "Davidoff is a faggot," he'd assert, more or less out of thin air, or "I hear that cocksucker Stevens is boffing both his secretaries. When the Nympho finds out, she'll have a vaginal collapse." Homer was an equal opportunity offender when it came to others' proclivities—though "cocksucker" was a term reserved exclusively for heterosexuals. Ethnicity wasn't one of his primary categories of derision, but he did enjoy poking fun at the "piece of fluff" that Gerald Bourne had brought over from Paris on his most recent annual visit (Gerald always showed up with a foulard for Homer, an extravagant scarf for Sally, and a tie for Paul, picked up, no doubt, at the Hermès airport gift shop). "What was *It* wearing?" the boss would ask, about someone whose sexuality was a little too fluid according to his antediluvian standards.

"I don't believe people do all the things you say they do, Homer; they couldn't possibly," Paul would object when Homer cataloged the shenanigans of his foes, and friends, to which Homer would counter, "No, but they do something." Which was hard to deny. Sexual activity for Homer was an index of moral fallibility and vitality at one and the same time. It didn't matter what people did; he was sure they did something illicit. It meant they were alive, like him. Maybe he was simply looking for companionship in transgression.

Homer had been a varsity sexual athlete in his prime, according to Georges Savoy, who told Paul that Stern would often return from lunch with wet hair. For years he had a special "wire" in his office, originally installed, it was rumored, for secret government contacts. Now, though, the old black rotary phone rang only when a woman friend from out of Homer's colorful past checked in; then Sally would stand in the hall and intone, "Your *phone* is ringing." (She refused to answer it herself.) Homer was reputed to have maintained a pied-à-terre near the office where he would repair for nooners, sometimes allegedly three-ways recruited (but how?) from among the staff. Sex was P & S's best—indeed its only—sport (the softball team was famously terrible), and it was Homer who set the tone. "Put this in with your smalls," he'd tell his rights director, Cherry Withington, on her way to Frankfurt, tossing her the galleys of a new book. Sex was recreation for him, a healthy, immensely satisfying pastime, and he was an avid tennis player too, well into his eighties. For all his profanity and bedroom antics, though, Homer was a relative prude when it came to misbehaving on the page. He was no Barney Rosset, the swashbuckling, boundary-testing founder of Grove Press, who'd braved the censorship laws bringing out *Lady Chatterley's Lover, The Story of O*, and other lubricious classics. Sex scenes in the novels Homer published made him uncomfortable, though he was convinced (erroneously, for the most part) that they sold books.

Paul could tell who Homer's old flames had been by how courtly he was with them, loyal in a way he was with no one else—not authors, relations, or even his best foreign confederates. Sex with Homer seemed to lead to friendship, perhaps the most unambivalent relationships he had. He was a ladies' man, and not just in the accepted sense of the term. Women seemed to offer him a solace that was missing from his noisy yet inarticulate sparring with men.

It was impossible for Homer to be really close to another male; his Neanderthal instinct was too strong. He boasted about his affection for his authors, the Three Aces in particular, but when Paul joined them for lunch, as he was always invited to because Homer, he sensed, was uncomfortable one-on-one, the conversation often ended up being superficial, if not inane—a terrible waste when three of the leading writers in the world were sitting at the table. Homer, for all his impact, was a man of a few words, many of them unprintable, which got repeated over and over in ingenious combinations. "And so forth and so on" was how his stories tended to trail off, with a dismissive wave. "Let's go make a book" was how he brought lunch to a close.

What Homer thrived on most was having enemies. Nothing gave him more pleasure than cutting dead a former employee—a "deserter," hence a nonperson—or providing a denigrating comment about a competitor to *The Daily Blade*. In his days doing army PR he'd learned that it didn't matter what you said as long as you were quoted. He had a series of rubber stamps for unwelcome correspondence, which he'd return with GREAT MOMENTS IN LITERATURE, HORSESHIT PIE, or best of all FUCK YOU VERY MUCH smudged in big black letters across the pages. He delighted in accusing Sandy Isenberg, the pint-sized president of Owl House, of boorishness, making bellicose public sallies that left Sandy, a short man unaccustomed to opposition of any kind, sputtering with rage.

Best of all, though, was fighting with agents, those parasites who interfered with his private relations with his property—i.e., his authors. Paul, who felt it was advisable to get along with people if possible because you might want or need to do business with them in the future, now and again suggested it might be politic to reestablish relations with Agent X, who had incurred Homer's ire years ago by selling a book he'd wanted to Farrar, Straus or Knopf.

"Don't give me that Christian forgiveness bullshit, Dukach. I'm a vindictive Jew!" he'd bellow. "End of joke!"—another classic Homer Stern way of closing a conversation.

One agent who loomed in his imagination was Angus McTaggart, with whom Homer enjoyed a long-standing sadomasochistic bromance. McTaggart, who professed to adore Homer, adored working his way through Homer's catalog even more, signing up his unrepresented or badly represented writers and then demanding oversize improvements in their compensation for their next books, which Homer delighted in being outraged about. Most of the writers ended up staying, on terms that made publishing them unprofitable for Homer, but some of the bigger ones did occasionally leave for greener pastures, like Abe Burack, after he finally hit it big with his big Brooklyn novel, *A Patch on Bernie*. Homer would thunder and swear and refuse to take Angus's calls for a few weeks or months. Then Angus would take him out to lunch, grovel apologetically, and pick up the check, an unheard-of deviation from the publisher-agent quadrille, and the cycle would start up again. But unlike the Nympho, another powerful agent who couldn't help taking Homer's acting-out personally (to be fair, there was a misogynist cast to many of his jabs), Angus reveled in the ritualized combat that was a way of averting boredom for both of them.

Homer loved winning, and loved seeing others lose even more. But he also enjoyed the game for its own sake. And he was extraordinarily good at it. He had created a highly articulated organism and employed the diversionary color of his personality effectively in its service—unless he got carried away, as he quite often did, by his emotions. His employees felt to him like his "illegitimate children"; they were the best in the business because they were his. He was no intellectual and didn't pretend to be, though he read, or "sniffed," as he put it, all the books he published. He was an amateur, in the original sense of the word: he loved writing and writers. And he was unmatched at the one thing that mattered to them more than anything—even money: he could get them talked about.

Now, having more or less recovered from his agon with the notebooks, Paul mentioned to Homer and Sally that he was rereading Pepita's demolishing essay on Outerbridge in *Retrospective Transgressions*, her scathing study of postwar Communist intellectuals. Pepita had become the darling of *The Protagonist*, the anti-Stalinist left-wing review, early in her career, when they'd published "Jiving with Joe," her exposé of the totalitarian principles that underlay Movement aesthetics, which had put her on the map as the nerviest cultural critic of her generation.

"I met Outerbridge in Venice," Homer was saying, rehearsing the story Paul had heard time and again. "Celine was his landlady. I was there the night he saw Ida again, ten years after their first affair. He was sitting on the Marino Marini in the courtyard—with the cock detached, naturally—drunk as usual. But still a good-looking man in his sixties—not quite an alter kocker. Too bad nobody reads him anymore." Homer's evil grin was a wonder to behold.

"I wouldn't quite say that, Homer," Paul demurred. "But what about Ida? Did you try to get her to come to us? Not just then but—"

"Is the pope Catholic?" Homer interrupted. "What self-respecting publisher wouldn't—though most of these pischikers can't tell their ass from their elbow. But Ida has always been loyal to Wainwright—though she did promise that if she ever made a change, she'd come to me."

Paul had heard that before; it was the oldest line in the business. But a man can dream, can't he? And this was one dream he and Homer shared. Having Ida at P & S would be an enormous coup for them both. He wondered if it could ever happen. He shouldn't even be thinking about it; the mere thought was disloyal to Sterling. But he was a publisher, wasn't he?

A few days later, as if on the spur of the moment, he put

in a call to Ida's agent, Roz Horowitz, a canny old bird who he felt had always had a soft spot for him, and asked her to lunch.

"So tell me about Ida Perkins, Roz. What's the news?" Paul asked, as they sipped their white wine at Bruno's, the overpriced midtown watering hole favored by the big publishers before they made their mass exodus to lower Manhattan in the mid- to late teens. On this particular afternoon Knopf's editorial whiz Jas Busbee, one of the banes of Paul's existence, was having lunch with the Nympho in one corner, while in the back of the room Angus McTaggart was leaning over the table whispering conspiratorially to his new client, Orin Roden, no doubt plotting about how to move him from P & S to Owl House or somewhere with even bigger pockets (as would soon happen), waving to Paul all the while. "You know she's always been my favorite poet."

"Get in line, dollink." Roz was a diminutive butterball of a woman whose legs didn't quite reach the floor when she was sitting in her chair. She had several chins and a large pile of hennaed hair pinned on top of her head, oversize sunglasses, and wore bright red lipstick. "That and a nickel will buy you exactly nothing. Ida Perkins is *everybody's* favorite poet, and you know it."

"Well, not quite everyone's. I never understood why she and Elspeth Adams were so standoffish."

"You didn't? I thought you said you knew poets. They

have their cliques and their claques, their jealousies and their sworn enmities, like all artists. If you go for Stravinsky you're not going to be too popular with Schoenberg. Take that bastard Hummock. He's always talking down his so-called friend Roden over there. It's human nature."

"I suppose you're right. Sometimes I think it's visceral, biological even. As if they can't stand each other's smell."

"Watch it, kiddo. Ida Perkins doesn't smell. She's as pure as a rose."

"I know she's perfect, Roz. And not only because she's your client. I yield to no one in my admiration of Ida Perkins. But a rose does have a wonderful, rich odor—and thorns, too, the last time I checked. I bet even the perfect Ida Perkins has had her . . . dissatisfactions over the years. How happy is she with her publisher?"

Roz gave Paul an even stare. "You know very well she's been with your new best buddy Sterling Wainwright more or less her whole life."

"Yes, of course. I wouldn't dream of interfering with a blissful relationship. I was just curious about how it's gone. From her perspective."

"The usual ups and downs. But I'm not sure I can imagine Ida anywhere else."

"Of course not." Paul retreated to his previous line of questioning. "Have you ever discussed Ms. Perkins's work with your sister?"

"Aren't we curious today. Hebe and I don't talk business. We've got enough to contend with dealing with our aged parents—and each other. I know she thinks the world of Ida, though; everyone with any taste does. I wouldn't be surprised if she wrote a book about her someday. I don't think she's so sure about Elizabeth Adams."

"Elspeth."

"If you say so. How pretentious can you get," Roz muttered under her breath before ordering herself another glass.

"Blame her parents if you must. I think it's a beautiful name myself. But getting back to Ms. Perkins—she hasn't published for quite a few years now. How is her health?"

"Fine, as far as I know. To tell you the truth, we're not in daily contact. You're aware she lives in Venice. And she's not on e-mail."

"Yes. I've been talking to Sterling about her and Arnold Outerbridge, working on these strange notebooks he left behind. They're written in a kind of code. I'd be interested in finding out what Ms. Perkins knows about them."

"Arnold Outerbridge! Did I ever tell you about my night with Arnold Outerbridge? What a shit! But that's a story for another time. What were you saying about these notebooks? Are you going to publish them?"

"That would be up to Sterling," Paul answered in his most self-effacing vein. "Right now we're simply trying to figure out what they add up to—if anything." Sterling and Paul had pored over Paul's transcription before he'd left Hiram's Corners, but Sterling hadn't had any better idea than Paul what was going on in them.

Roz sipped her wine and assessed Paul silently. At last she said, "Listen—I have an idea. Why don't you go pay Ida a visit after Frankfurt? I'll arrange it."

"Do you think she'd see me? That would be fantastic, Roz! I don't know how to thank you."

"Just remember you can't talk poetry with her. She detests literary types. And suck-ups."

"Roz! I promise I won't forget."

"Don't. Because if you start going la-di-da on her, you're toast."

"I give you my word."

They finished their double decaf espressos and Paul paid for their lunch (two salades niçoises and Roz's three glasses of Falanghina to his one), planted a noisy kiss on each cheek, and put her into a taxi. He rode the bus down Fifth Avenue to give himself time to daydream a little. He couldn't keep from fantasizing about what it would be like to be in Ida's presence, to actually hear her speak. He was half afraid that when she did open her mouth, he'd be so overwhelmed that what she said would go in one ear and out the other and he'd come away with nothing but the memory of his own fascination.

Yes, he had an ulterior motive in making his visit, he admitted to himself as the bus crawled through the afternoon traffic past the Empire State Building, into the seedier stretches of the Garment District and Koreatown, and on past the Flatiron Building. And Roz was well aware of it; she was setting it up, wasn't she? What he really wanted, though, was simply to be in Ida's presence, to see how she moved, to hear the sound of her voice. Whatever happened beyond that, if anything, would be gravy.

The bus lurched to a halt at Fourteenth Street, and he made his escape. He was going to see Ida Perkins in Venice. Unaccountably, he was convinced this visit would change his life. First though, he had to get through Frankfurt.

VIII

The Fair

The modern-day Frankfurt Book Fair was a postwar phenomenon, a vehicle for easing the readmission of Germany into the company of civilized Western societies. Originally, it had been a phenomenon of the Renaissance, Frankfurt being the largest trading center near Mainz, where Johannes Gutenberg and his fellows had invented movable type in the late 1430s. The fair had been established again in 1949 and had grown into the most important annual gathering in international publishing. Every October, tens of thousands of publishers from all over the world scurried like so many ants among the warehouse-like halls of the fair's bleak campus on the edge of the city center, rushing to appointments with their counterparts.

But books weren't sold at the modern-day Frankfurt. Authors were—by the pound and sometimes by the gross. What the publishers did at Frankfurt was hump the right to sell their writers' work in other territories and languages, often pocketing a substantial portion of the earnings for themselves (the ever-paternalistic French were among the most egregious, raking off 50 percent of the take). The days before agents woke up to the potential of international deals were a wild and woolly era, though the seigneurial rituals of fair commerce were punctiliously observed by the players. Rights directors were the most visible players under the Frankfurt bell jar, and the acknowledged queen of them all was Cora Blamesly, FSG's mace-wielding Iron Maiden, who hailed from the arbor-draped hills of Carinthia and was a past master at brandishing her picked-up Sloane Ranger accent, with its ineradicable Germanic undertone, and her S/M selling techniques to extract outrageous contracts from her desperate European "friends."

Cora and her ilk would hold back important manuscripts for sale at the fair and then "slip" them with elaborate fanfare to favored editors in various territories, demanding that they be read overnight and soliciting preemptive offers, often inflated by the expectations and tensions of Frankfurt's carnival atmosphere.

The Europeans were desperate because the postwar cultural economy had dictated that Italian and German, Japanese and Brazilian, and sometimes even French readers needed and wanted to read American books. Not just the big commercial authors, either, the Stephen Kings and Danielle Steels, but the Serious Literary Writers, too. First there'd been the anxiety-ridden, attitude-infused Jewish American novelists; followed by the less interesting, more self-regarding WASPs, the Updikes and Styrons and Foxxes; and the nondescript newbies, the young Turks full of sass and plausibility that Cora and her counterparts whipped up into supernovas for the four days of the fair, sometimes for book after book, year after year. European publishing nabobs like Jorge Vilas (Spain), Norberto Beltraffio (Italy), Matthias Schoenborn (Germany), and the biggest overspender of them all, Danny van Gennep from Utrecht, had been playing this way for years, and were on the hook to Cora for literal millions. When Roger Straus or Lucy Morello brought a new author to Frankfurt, they all jumped, as they did for Rob Routman, the head-turning editor in chief of Owl House—sometimes, it was rumored, without reading all that much (or, let's be honest, any) of the manuscript—because often, or often enough anyway, the books "worked," i.e., sold copies back home. Many publishers played "Ready, Fire, Aim" buying foreign books, acquiring titles that sounded hot but often, when the commissioned translations materialized months later, would have them shaking their heads, wondering how such a dog could have appeared so leonine in the half-light of the smoke-infested Hessischer Hof bar, still packed at two a.m. with drunken, libidinous editors and rights people splayed across each other on the sagging couches.

The serial drink dates and *langweilisch* alcoholic dinners with self-congratulatory speeches by the hosting German publishers, followed by more drinks on into the night (same-time-next-year cohabitation was not unheard of, either) contributed to Frankfurt's nonstop bonhomie and its open-walleted frenzy. As one grand old man of Danish publishing had told Homer, "We come to Frankfurt every year to see if we're still alive." Some, alas, were not. The worst were former bigwigs who had the bad taste to reappear, wandering the cavernous halls, buttonholing former colleagues between nonexistent appointments. They were ghosts, revenants, and everyone knew it—including them, perhaps.

Frankfurt was anything but social; it was carnivorousness at its most rapacious, with a genteel European veneer. The dressy clothes, the parties, the cigars, the jacked-up prices in the hotels and restaurants, the disappointing food were all of a piece. It was exhausting and repetitive and depressing—and no one in publishing with any sense or style would have missed it for the world.

Homer was made for Frankfurt. Nowhere was he more relaxed, more full of avuncular wisdom and wisecracking anecdotes. He had refused to come to postwar Germany for years, but had been won over by Brigitta Bohlenball, the vivacious widow of Friedrich Bohlenball, who had almost instantaneously, thanks to a series of shrewd buys, used his Swiss milk fortune and Communist politics (a Swiss Communist: a rara avis indeed!) to become one of Europe's most stylish publishers. Friedrich had introduced a number of weighty novelists and philosophers before committing suicide at the age of forty, leaving Brigitta and young Friedchen with several hundred million Swiss francs, a villa near Lugano, and a *Schloss* in the Engadine, not to mention Zurich's swankiest publishing house.

"Come, Homer. You'll have such a good time, I promise you," Brigitta cooed over lunch at La Caravelle, and she'd made good on her vow, introducing her new American catch to the greatest, which is to say the most snobbish, editors in Europe.

If a snobbish publisher seems like an oxymoron today, it's only an indication of how the notion of class has degraded in the postwar era. The aristocrats of European publishing, the Gallimards, Einaudis, and Rowohlts, were good old bourgeois who had gotten through the war more or less intact, though sometimes with not-unblemished political affiliations in their back pockets, as was true for numberless European businessmen. They weren't very different, mutatis mutandis, from Homer, which is no doubt why he came to feel so at home among them. And he did feel gloriously, chest-thumpingly himself in those smoky, cold fair halls and smoky, overheated hotel bars and restaurants. Membership in Brigitta's club had long since stilled his qualms about the Krauts, as he still called them, and the saturnalia of Frankfurt had become the high point of Homer's and Sally's publishing year.

They appeared as a couple, and indeed many of Homer's foreign colleagues, some of whom enjoyed not-dissimilar domestic arrangements, thought they were married. Paul remembered a dinner at Homer's town house soon after he'd joined the company with a number of P & S's better-known foreign authors, including Piergiorgio Ponchielli and his wife, Anita Moreno, and Marianne O'Loane. Norberto Beltraffio, one of Homer's most exuberant European colleagues, sailed into the drawing room while Homer was seeing to the wine and, throwing his arms wide, asked the assembled crowd, "Where's Sally?" Luckily, Iphigene was also out of the room.

As a rule, Homer and Sally spent a long weekend at a spa on Lake Constance, resting up for the ardors of the fair, and afterward flew on to London or Paris to recover in style for a week or two. They were gone for a month's vacation, as some back in New York had it, and on the company dime.

Over the years, he'd come to be seen by many as the dean of Frankfurt's gang of literary publishers, "the King of the fair," as Brigitta had crowned him. His engagement in its rites, his small dinner at the fair's end every year, for which some leading European publishers stayed late, his charm and mode of dress, which fit right in here and didn't feel extravagant or slightly garish as it could in New York, even his contraband Cuban cigars—all added to Homer's stature in the halls and watering holes of Frankfurt. The Spartan P & S booth, which echoed his no-frills offices in New York, was tacked onto a large international distributor's stand and overflowed with visitors from all over Europe, Latin America, and Asia, come to kiss the gold seal ring on Homer's well-veined hand.

There were other Frankfurts going on simultaneously that Homer and Sally and Paul, who had been attending with them for the past few years, had nothing to do with. The Big (i.e., irrelevant commercial) Publishers, the Random Houses and HarperCollinses and Simon & Schusters and Hachettes, wheeled and dealt multimillion-dollar contracts among themselves, though increasingly the agents were holding on to their authors' foreign rights, stalking the halls and booths like hyenas, or even, egregiously, like the upstart McTaggart, setting up their own stands with spiffy little tables and printed catalogs several inches thick handed out by demure young people, aping the publishers themselves (the nerve!). And then there was the religious publishers' Frankfurt; the techies' and scientists' Frankfurt; the illustrated book publishers' Frankfurt; the university press publishers' Frankfurt; the developing world publishers' Frankfurt. Not to mention the hosting German publishers' Frankfurt, which was not just for one-on-one publisher-to-publisher deal making, but for the authors, the critics and journalists—believe it or not, books and writers were still news in Germany—and, after the first couple of days, the public, too. They gawked and dawdled like the tourists they were, till the aisles were virtually impassable.

All these fairs, and others, too, were going on at the same time in the same cavernous spaces, which were like the biggest big-box stores ever built, their denizens streaming into the fairgrounds, riding half-mile-long mobile walkways, hitching rides on commuter trains from the beautiful old central railway station so evocative for Paul of prewar Europe, drinking late into the night in the dangerously crowded lobbies of the hotels, hungover and sleepless and hoarse by day, complaining and fibbing and wheedling and smoking and drinking, gorging and lying and drinking and fucking by night, and having the time of their lives.

To the literary publishers, however, Frankfurt was theirs and theirs alone. They set the tone; they published the Authors Who Mattered—and who sometimes unwisely showed up for receptions and speeches, though those with any self-awareness soon realized they were irrelevant encumbrances to the business at hand. The literary publishers were the Lords of Culture, the master parasites sitting on top of this swarming dunghill. Their sense of their own importance showed when they walked the halls, rolling from side to side as if they were on board an ocean liner—which in a sense they were, without knowing it: a slow-moving Ship of Fools behemoth, heading willy-nilly for the great big digital iceberg. They convened in gemütlich private receptions to which the riffraff were not invited (exclusive invitations were a ritual of the fair, sent out months in advance and occasionally even coveted). They eyed each other sharply but unobtrusively as they fibbed about their latest finds, which might conceivably be but most of the time emphatically were not the Major Contributions to World Literature they aimed to pass them off as. The pros among these gentlemanly thieves understood each other perfectly: where amity ended and commerce held sway; where commerce took a backseat and long loyalty asserted its claims. Homer was widely generous with his information, be it good or bad, and he was a past master at spreading the rumors that were the lifeblood of Frankfurt: that McTaggart was moving Hummock from Gallimard to Actes Sud; that Hummock had dumped McTaggart for the Nympho; that the Nympho was selling her agency to William Morris lock, stock, and barrel.

Homer would make special deals to keep certain authors within the inner circle—the *cénacle*, or cartel, some might call it—of independent houses that was informally run by him and his partners in crime. It was old-fashioned horse-trading, sure, but it often proved salutary for the authors, for over time, if they truly had the stuff (and some of them did; if not, the whole house of cards would have collapsed long ago), their international stature would gradually mature, and their readership would inevitably spread like their publishers' waistlines.

Quite a few of Homer's authors—more than from any other American house except FSG, a constant thorn in his side—had ended up with the Big One, the Giant Kahuna, the platinum standard in World Literature, the highest of stakes, for which he was always playing: the Nobel Prize in Literature, awarded by the hypersecretive Swedish Academy. In the United States, the Nobel didn't quite have the commercial heft it did elsewhere, but its prestige was still unparalleled. In recent years Homer had taken to raking in Nobels the way some collect watches. Seven of the last twelve literature prizes had gone to P & S authors, to the disgruntlement of many. Homer had been heard to boast that he was on familiar terms with the king of Sweden, whose major duty seemed to be handing out the Nobel medals.

The prize was traditionally announced on the Thursday of the fair at one p.m., during the frenetic lunch hour. The big cheeses were far too suave to stand around waiting for the announcement; nevertheless, their underlings knew how to reach them at the all-important moment. This year, for the first time in decades, Homer hadn't come to Frankfurt; he was having a hip replacement that couldn't be postponed, and Sally had stayed home to help nurse him. So Paul was there on his own to carry the flag, gingerly treading in his boss's oversize footsteps through the set-in-stone routine of meetings and receptions, trying not to appear like the underdressed hick he felt he must be taken for by Homer's cliquish crowd.

In 2010, as had been the case for the past few years, Ida Perkins was rumored to be on the short list for the Nobel. How accurate such speculation was, was anybody's guess. The putatively short-listed candidates—nobody knew if there actually *was* a short list—often failed to emerge as winners; and if a writer was mentioned year after year, she or he could become stale goods, even less likely to garner the ultimate accolade than the dark horses—though stale goods could miraculously become fresh-baked overnight and end up winning, as had happened more than once. This year Ida, who at eighty-four had entered Now or Never territory, was again being actively discussed as a potential winner: it was time for an American, a woman, a poet: why not all three in one?

"Now you must tell me, Paul," whined Maria Mariasdottir, who'd cornered him one evening in the Frankfurter Hof bar, a suite of spacious rooms furnished with lots of, but never enough, sofas and chairs on the ground floor of Hitler's favorite hotel, though it was larger and dowdier than the more exclusive Hessischer Hof across town. At night the Frankfurter Hof became an even sweatier, smokier mosh pit than the Hessischer Hof, so packed with literary flesh peddlers you could barely move. Paul thought of it as the third circle of Hell.

"Who," Maria kept asking, "is this Ida Perkins?"

Maria was a hardworking, sloe-eyed, shapely young publisher from Reykjavik who often appealed to her fellow publishers in other territories for tips since she couldn't afford the staff to read most of the books submitted to her.

"Ida Perkins is to American poetry as Proust is to the French novel. Seriously." Paul recoiled internally hearing himself talking Frankfurt-speak, a repulsive commercial shorthand he loathed yet had developed a disgusting facility with—even when it came to Ida; though she wasn't "his" author, he felt compelled to spread the word about her at every opportunity. It was nearing midnight, long past his normal witching hour, but the crowd was just beginning to thicken like a rancid sauce. He knew he'd had far too much to drink and needed to get back to his two-star hotel in the red-light district near the Hauptbahnhof.

"Yes, but is she *really* good? I mean *really*, *really*, *really* good? I need to know."

"Yes, Maria, Ida is *really*, *really*, *really* good—absolutely the top. I'm telling you it's true—and we don't even publish her, alas."

"Are you sure, because translating her will be so difficult, so expensive . . ."

"Maria, I don't know your market. All I know is that Ida

Perkins is *the* American poet of our time. And her work is going to last. Ask Matthias Schoenborn if you don't believe me. He's bringing out her *Collected* next year. Ask Beltraffio. Ask Jean-Marie Groddeck. They're all convinced." The fact that certain prestigious publishers had an author on their lists often carried irrational weight with their foreign colleagues.

"Yes, but is she *really, really* good?"

"*Really, really, really* good, Maria. Really." He hoped he wasn't slurring his words, but feared he just might be.

"I'm doubtful," she said.

Paul threw up his hands and planted a smooch on the nonplussed Maria's forehead (most Europeans were deft practitioners of the air kiss, where lips never touched skin, but Americans often failed to carry it off). At least Maria really, really wanted to know if Ida was worth translating. The truth was, what was hot in New York was often dead on arrival in Reykjavik, and vice versa—that was the terrible truth, and maybe the saving grace, of international publishing. Paul sometimes had reason to wish there were a Frankfurt morning-after pill; but a deal was a deal, even one shaken on when one of the parties—or, better, both—was two or three sheets to the wind.

So Paul was feeling cautious when he sat down in Homer's stead at Matthias Schoenborn's table in the German hall the next morning for their annual discussion—lecture might have been a better word—about Matthias's prizewinning, best-selling Mitteleuropean authors. If Homer had been there, he and Matthias, who were mad about each other, would have spent their half hour telling off-color jokes and denigrating their closest collaborators, as happy as pigs in shit, but Paul knew he would have to settle for an actual business meeting. Experience told him that few or none of the writers Matthias would be pitching were likely to make an impact in America, just as he knew in his heart of hearts that Matthias, who was one of the shrewdest showboats among the international publishers, much admired for his ebullience and his nonstop promoting of his writers—a kind of latter-day European version of Homer—had no deep interest in the authors Homer and Paul published. Sure, Matthias would grumble about the fact that Eric Nielsen, now an enormous international presence, was published by Friedchen Bohlenball, though Matthias hadn't shown the slightest interest when Paul had buttonholed him excitedly about his discovery years ago. The truth was, Matthias didn't care about what Paul was doing any more than Paul cared about Matthias's Russian and Iranian émigrés eking out an existence as cabbies in Berlin. Still, they sat and talked animatedly every year—"He lies to me and I lie to him," as Homer put it—and went to each other's parties and were the best of Frankfurt pals, listening all the while for signs in each other's cascading verbiage of that rarest of things, the world-class author who could make a difference for both of them. How to listen, Paul had come to feel, was the real test of Homer's publishing "truffle hound." Many, unfortunately, listened only to themselves.

Still, over the years, Matthias and Homer and now Paul had shared certain core writers who had had an international impact, among them Homer's Three Aces. And Matthias, a respected avant-garde writer himself (Homer had published several of his dark, abstruse short novels before giving up the ghost), was Ida's German publisher, too, and he was well aware of Paul's passion for her and her work. Being the canny insider he was, Matthias often seemed to have privileged information about deliberations in Stockholm, and this year was no exception.

"It's possible," he told Paul. "There are other currents afoot, but it's possible."

Paul didn't know what to make of these gnomic tea leaves. All he could do was what everyone else was doing: wait.

He was at the booth at one o'clock, but the silence was deafening. After an excruciating wait, word went around that Hendrijk David of the Netherlands had squeaked out enough votes to take the prize. It was said he'd been expecting it for years, sitting complacently by the phone on the appointed morning each October.

The rumor, though, turned out to be erroneous. Dries

van Meegeren, another, far more obscure Dutch essayist, had won, setting off an unseemly free-for-all for the acquisition of his largely still-available rights. Publishers from nearly everywhere, who before today had never heard of van Meegeren, swarmed the normally empty Dutch hall, anxious to buy themselves a Nobel Prize winner. The booth of De Bezige Bij, The Busy Bee, van Meegeren's lucky publisher, resembled a rebooking desk in an airline terminal after a canceled flight. (David, meanwhile, never recovered, dying in bitter disappointment a couple of years later.)

In any case, the prize hadn't gone to Ida. Paul consoled himself with the fact that her not having won meant she still could.

He phoned Homer once the office was open in New York.

"Can you believe Dries won?" he cackled, giddy with disbelief. Van Meegeren had been campaigning for the Nobel for ages, going on reading tours across Scandinavia, writing articles about the work of Swedish Academy members, even taking up with a Swedish woman reputed to be on a first-name basis with the academy's secretary.

"That gonif has been kissing Swedish ass for years," Homer answered. "I was hoping for Les or Adam. I need my Four of a Kind, you know."

"It will happen, Homer. All in good time. Everyone

here sends love." Paul relayed greetings from a passel of Homer's long-standing confreres.

"Keep your nose clean and have fun. I'll see you Monday."

"Not Monday. Remember, I'm going to visit Ida Perkins in Venice after the fair."

"Right." Paul could hear Homer clearing his throat across the ocean. "Well, give her a slap on the ass for me, and tell her our arms are always open. Keep me posted!"

"Will do—at least the second and third parts," Paul answered, and rang off. The fair had another two days to run, but he could hardly wait for it to be over. He sleep-walked through his appointments and forced himself to put in an appearance at a few receptions, trying to muster the enthusiasm to host the firm's Friday night dinner in Homer's stead. He couldn't help feeling that, like him, Homer's pals would be on autopilot without their Fearless Leader to mirror back their well-rehearsed performances as cultural grandees—marshals of France, someone called them. Self-importance was ubiquitous, Paul knew, but there was a particular smarmy pungency to the horse-trading in Frankfurt that he found revolting, especially when he was engaging in it. It was a far cry from the poetry of Ida Perkins or the novels of Ted Jonas, sweated out in anguish and solitude. The idea of Ida or Eric Nielsen or Pepita here among these overdressed, overfed word merchants who acted as if they owned their writers' hides made him faintly ill.

On Friday evening he stood in his off-the-rack suit at a long table in an otherwise deserted hotel restaurant as Homer's crowd—Brigitta, Norberto, Matthias, Beatriz, Jorge and Lalli, Héloise, Gianni, Teresa—sat expectantly, waiting, he was sure, for him to commit an unforced error. He made a stab at imitating Homer's offhand delivery of one of his risqué toasts, but Paul's own attempts at public humor usually came off a little forced. All seemed to be going along all right, though, until he made the mistake of mentioning e-books:

"Why, before you know it, you'll be enjoying Padraic and Thor and Pepita and Dmitry on your own devices, just like us!" he exclaimed with ersatz jollity, given that he'd never opened an e-reader himself.

It was as if he'd farted at the table or mentioned the Holocaust. Brigitta and Matthias stared at each other bug-eyed and sucked in their cheeks, like specters out of Goya's *Disasters of War*, imagining the digital horde advancing from the West like the latest strain of American influenza. Thank God they would be too old to care when it reached their shores.

Paul shrank down in his seat. What would Homer and Sally say when word reached them, as it assuredly would, that he'd demonstrated once and for all how unsuited he was for this well-padded, backward-looking world?

He couldn't wait to breathe the fetid air of his beloved Venice, where he often escaped after the mind-numbing hothouse of the fair. He washed down the rest of his veal chop with too much syrupy *Rotwein*, ushered his last guests out of the funereal restaurant, and caught the midnight train with minutes to spare. He arrived in Venice early the next morning, sleepless but jangly with excitement.

He splurged on a water taxi down the Grand Canal, stunned as always to be confronted with how truly strange Venice was. The shut-up palaces fell straight into the oily loden-colored water (what held them up?). The sky alternated between pearlescent and Bellini blue. He felt gusts of enchantment and resistance, elation and revulsion. Venice was a hallucinatory incubus, the most artificial environment in the world: Disneyland for grown-ups. It reeked of sex and its putrescent partner, death. Thomas Mann had caught its rouged, feverish aura perfectly.

What was Ida Perkins, the avatar of red-cheeked American expansiveness and optimism, doing here? This was a place to hide, to fade away—not to grab life by the lapels, as she always had. Had Ida become infected by A.O.'s old man's despondency? Or had she found a new lease on life with Leonello Moro? Was Ida still Ida?

Paul spent the morning wandering, struck yet again

by the seemingly chance beauty of Italian public spaces, shaken down over time into nonchalant irregularity and aptness. He had always felt lighter in Italy, unburdened by expectations, his own or anyone else's; he could move at will here, unimpeded and unobserved, as he sometimes could in New York, too, actually, walking anonymous in the noontime crowd. He had lunch in the autumn sun at a trattoria in the Campo Santo Stefano, and made stabs at resuscitating his dormant Italian. He reread Ida's Venice book, *Aria di Giudecca*, which was as alive to the decay and incandescence of the city as anything he knew ("city of Jewish saints / of cul-de-sacs and feints / of stains and taints"). Then he started leafing through his transcriptions of A.O.'s notebooks while he sipped his espresso:

14 JUNE 1987

8:45 caffè latte, pane al cioccolato
10:15 Dr. Giannotti
14:30 computer
15:40 phone call—U.S.
16:20 Debenedetti
17:00 seamstress
20:00 Celine

hair heaven glimmer thread error reflect pillow binding

Seamstress? Why would Arnold see a seamstress? Paul shivered a little as the gathering shadows overtook the afternoon sun. Then he returned to his reading. On Monday he was going to meet Ida Perkins. He had lots of questions and he wanted to be prepared.

IX

Dorsoduro 434

The gloomy "false Byzantium" of the Hotel Danieli bar at three o'clock on an October afternoon was only partly offset by the blaze in the fireplace reflected in the room's high-hung, aged mirrors. The upholstery of the couches, gray *peau de soie* moiré, suited Paul's mood. Outside was burnished Venice autumn weather—pure cloudless blue, sixty-eight degrees in the sun on the Riva degli Schiavoni; but he was trapped inside, overcoat beside him on the couch, waiting for Ida Perkins.

He was taut and indrawn, the way he tended to be when meeting someone new, but especially so today. He was about to come face-to-face with the Person, the Goddess, the One and Only . . . he was winding himself up, he knew; he had to stop.

Why was he here? He had a sudden urge to hightail it back to New York and forget the whole thing. Instead, he played with his BlackBerry, scanning but not reading his messages.

Suddenly, a slender figure turned the corner from the foyer and peered into the mote-filled semi-gloom before making her way toward him, negotiating among the islands of furniture that filled the room.

Ida was here.

But no, it was an elderly Italian woman in a heavy pea jacket, not Ida at all.

"Signor Dukach, La Contessa Moro is not well today, *mi dispiace davvero*," the woman offered. "She asked me to see if instead you might come see her tomorrow afternoon."

"Yes, of course, ma'am. I can do that." Paul felt a thrill. He was going to visit Ida at home! Over the years on his trips to Venice, he'd scoped out her address, hoping for a glimpse of her in a window or, better yet, on the street. Now he was going to see for himself.

"*A che ora, signora?*" he asked, as nonchalantly as he could.

"*Alle quattro del pomeriggio, per piacere. Dorsoduro 434, presso San Gabriele. Grazie, grazie tante.*"

The woman looked around anxiously, rubbing her hands together as if from the cold, though the room was pleasantly warm. Nodding apologetically, she backed away, turned, and disappeared.

Paul was reprieved! He was going to see Ida, but not yet. Carefree, he strolled in the thinning light past the Arsenale, all the way to San Pietro di Castello; then he meandered back through a warren of backwater rios to San Marco and over the Accademia Bridge. After a stint in the museum with his favorite Carpaccios, he found his way to Montin, a simple trattoria on a de Chiricoesque canal where the maître d' was only too happy to show him the table where Ezra Pound had sat with his back to the crowd every evening with Olga Rudge—and occasionally, in his last years, with Arnold and Ida.

He had a couple of limoncellos after his *fegato alla veneziana* and polenta and then wandered back to his hotel on a small canal that gave onto the Giudecca, passing the monument to Dmitry Chavchavadze on the way. Dmitry, who had died of a heart attack in Atlanta a few years before, had, like other émigrés, chosen to spend his immortality in Venice, the ultimate way station of the exile.

Paul fell asleep immediately. In the morning, he lit out for the Ghetto and the farther reaches of Cannaregio with his dog-eared Red Guide, paying an obligatory visit on the way to barrel-vaulted Santa Maria dei Miracoli, nestled like a marble boat in the harbor of small canals surrounding her.

* * *

The nondescript entrance to Palazzo Moro di Schiuma fronted on a narrow alley that ended unceremoniously at the Grand Canal. Paul rang the bell at precisely 4:00 and a small door clicked open. After walking down a short brick passageway between high stucco walls with shards of broken bottles at the top, he found himself in a disused garden.

Climbing vines just losing their reddened leaves covered the back of the house. Paul entered the portico to the right as directed and took the small elevator to the fourth floor.

It opened onto a squarish marble entryway in which a tall, frail woman with pure white hair coiled on top of her head was leaning on a cane with a carved, yellowed ivory handle. She wore a stylishly cut brown wool shift, with no jewelry except a round brooch of rough gold, and brown velvet slippers.

Yes, Ida was still Ida, Paul surmised, taking her measure once he'd recovered from the shock of her presence. Her high cheekbones retained their almost Mongol glamour, though the skin was drawn thin across them.

"Come in, Mr. Dukach."

"Ms. Perkins, it is such an honor to meet you."

She half bowed and indicated a pair of couches in the middle of the room, then led him slowly to them, sitting facing him, with a tea table between them.

As he moved through the low-ceilinged room furnished with commodiously grouped, low-slung Venetian fauteuils and lit here and there in the failing daylight by Murano glass lamps glowing red and green like signal lights, Paul noticed a closed-in gallery at the far end, overlooking what had to be the Grand Canal. It was here he had read somewhere that Wagner had written the third act of *Tristan und Isolde.* The walls of the room were covered in beige damask, overhung not with the expected Venetian scenes but with paintings by Severini and Morandi and, to his delight, a surreal seascape, the largest and most captivating Paul had ever seen, by the Italian Post-Impressionist De Pisis. Where, he wondered, was Leonello Moro's notorious contemporary collection?

A few logs smoldered in a small fireplace near the door, and a lamp was lit on the desk near the east end of the room overlooking the gallery, where Ida had been working, or so it appeared.

"Would you like some tea, Mr. Dukach?" Ida's unreconstructed Brahmin accent, with its broad extended vowels, was out of another era.

He nodded distractedly. Being here was making him forget what he'd so carefully planned to say.

Ida rang a small bell on the table beside her. The woman from yesterday appeared.

"*Tè, per cortesia*, Adriana," Ida instructed her servant.

"So. Now how can I help you?" she asked, turning to Paul. She was firm, maybe a little brusque as she patted the pillows behind her back, making herself comfortable. Paul was surprised to find that instead of the expansiveness he'd endowed her with in his fantasies, the Ida in front of him was old-fashioned, restrained, no-nonsense. And guarded.

"Rosalind Horowitz, as I believe you know, suggested I

come see you," he began. "I'm working with Sterling Wainwright on Arnold Outerbridge's red notebooks. We're trying . . . well, *I'm* trying to figure them out."

"Oh yes." Ida nodded. "Roz wrote me all about you." She seemed to relax a bit. "And Sterling tells me you know more about me—about my work, anyway—than anyone, apart from him, of course. Which is more than a little frightening, I have to admit." Ida laughed an uncomfortable little laugh. "I've certainly never heard him talk that way about another publisher—and one who works for Homer Stern to boot!"

Ida turned her face toward him at a quizzical angle, as if expecting Paul to reveal himself. Could this really be Ida, the interlocutor of so many of his wishful dreams?

"Sterling has been incredibly kind. I've learned an unbelievable amount from him. And Homer asked to be remembered to you, of course. *He's* always talking about *you*."

"I can imagine," Ida answered with a bit of a chuckle. "How is dear old Homer? Still chasing the girls?"

"Well, probably not quite the way he used to. He's over eighty, you know."

"How impertinent of you to mention it, young man! As you're well aware, I'm even older!" To his relief, Paul saw that Ida was laughing openly now. He hadn't turned her off. Not yet.

"That's quite hard to believe." He managed to raise his eyes and meet hers, which were tautly focused on him, their legendary green undimmed.

"Anyway, as I was saying," Paul forged ahead, "I've been trying to help . . . Sterling decipher Outerbridge's notebooks in my spare time. I've made progress on the code he wrote them in. I know what they say. But what they mean is still a mystery. Roz thought you might be able to help—that you could tell me more about them."

The woman in gray appeared with a tea tray and set it on the table between them. Ida was silent as she poured out their tea: Lapsang souchong; he was almost drugged by its rich, smoky scent. She offered him milk, which he accepted, and sugar, which he refused. Then she looked up.

"So. You've read the notebooks . . ."

"Yes. They appear to be timekeeping notes of some sort. A diary of his daily activities. Very minute and . . ."

"And obsessional."

"Well, yes, in a word. As if he needed to keep track of his every movement."

"I see," Ida responded grimly, looking down into her lap. Then she raised her eyes, the lines in her tanned face deeply etched, and said carefully, "I'm afraid that in his last years, Arnold wasn't capable of working anymore. Which was terribly cruel, given how prolific, how totally absorbed in his writing, he'd always been."

"I'm very sorry," Paul said, lowering his eyes. There was silence before he added, "There's nothing worse than seeing a brilliant person deprived of his gifts."

Ida nodded.

"You were together a long time," Paul continued, trying to gently prime the pump.

"Nearly twenty years, this last go-around."

"I have to confess I always imagined you side by side, sharing your work, discussing ideas, inspiring each other."

"Well, I can see you haven't learned very much in your young years," Ida shot back derisively.

"Forgive me, Ms. Perkins, but I hope you can appreciate how large you and Mr. Outerbridge loom in the imaginations of some of us," he answered.

"You're not one of those despicable literary sleuths who thinks he can deduce every last little sordid biographical detail from a writer's work, are you?" Ida asked, with ill-concealed suspicion.

Paul sat back, flummoxed. Was that what he was?

Ida's jaw was set. Her eyes flared with indignation. "When, I want to know, do writers get to simply live their boring lives? Don't you know living is not about writing, Mr. Dukach? There was always so much else going on. Svetlana. The shopping. The laundry—and the doctors! Writing is something one does—we both *did*, I should say—to escape, to get away. And also maybe to make sense of one's mistakes, wrong turns you know you've made but can't come to terms with any other way. Poor man's psychoanalysis, Arnold used to call it.

"Arnold engaged with the world day in and day out. But he couldn't have cared less what was for dinner, or who was sleeping with whom. He always had his eye on the bigger picture."

"And you?" Paul ventured.

"My story was entirely different. I grew up in a sheltered environment, and felt the need to break away early on. Unlike Arnold, who endured deprivation from childhood. Sterling and I had to get away and see things for ourselves. It's what brought us together that summer in Michigan. All those sailors and croquet players swirling around us in the dining hall at Otter Creek, planning their tournaments and regattas, while we were plotting our escape—to New York, London, Paris."

Paul relaxed a little. Ida, he sensed, was performing one of her solos.

"We got there, too, each in our own way. We helped each other—at least he helped me, though my options as a woman were, needless to say, far more limited. When I published my first book it was a veritable scandal at Bryn Mawr! The shadow of Marianne Moore hung over the place like a cloying little modernist cloud. The atmosphere was far too claustrophobic for yours truly. And those intensely . . .

innocent crushes on each other. I was *not* innocent, or at least I didn't want to be. I wanted to be scandalous!"

Ida was enjoying herself.

"You certainly turned poetry on its head, from the very first," Paul said.

"I was a college sophomore, just having a little fun. But *they*—the literary folk—took me seriously. That was the last thing I was expecting—or wanting. Another regimen, with another set of rules and expectations."

"How did it feel to be the toast of the town when you were still a teenager?"

"Those silly young/old men with their unreadable magazines and their precious self-importance. Little prigs! I've always despised the Establishment, Paul, and that includes the Bohemian Establishment, which is really no different from the bankers. Poetry, for me, and for everyone serious, I think, is about otherness: being 'maladjusted,' standing apart. They didn't understand the first thing about what I was writing—or what was happening to me."

Ida leaned back and coughed a little. Her superfine hair was spun sugar in the lamplight.

"Then I met Barry Saltzman. He seemed like the way out—he was dashing, open, mature, supportive, generous. He was quite a bit older, and it didn't bother him one bit that I was a writer—an outré one, even. He was proud of my 'independence.' He thought he was encouraging it. We had a lovely apartment in the East Seventies and I had maids and a secretary and all the time in the world to work. I just didn't have anything to write *about*—do you understand? I needed experience. I needed to *derange my senses*."

Ida looked up, as if to gauge whether he was following her. Paul nodded encouragement.

"And there was ravishing Sterling again, hanging around the Village with people Barry wouldn't have known how to talk to. Sterling took me everywhere, including to his apartment more than once, I'm not ashamed to say, and . . . but"—Ida looked toward the windows—"I'm boring you."

"You have to be joking! Nothing could be further from the truth."

Her skin was nearly translucent. Ida trembled faintly at times as she continued.

"Then Stephen came along, Stephen Roentgen, at one of those insufferable Fifty-seventh Street art gallery readings. My quondam suitor Delmore Schwartz was there, still more or less compos mentis, and John Berryman, and old Wallace Stevens, too, down from Hartford, the one time I met him, still complaining about Eliot, if you can believe it. That's when that pig Ora Troy started acting up, accusing me of poaching. Always out for attention. But Stephen, who was fresh off the boat from Liverpool, was pure genius—wild-eyed, extravagant, and a wonderful poet. Yes, he'd known Ora; but it was love at first sight—for both of us. No doubt you've seen the pictures of him with his shirt front unbuttoned and that dreamy wave in his hair. Stephen had such verve—and intensity, commitment, talent, belief in himself. He just didn't have staying power."

Ida was looking across the tea table straight at him. Paul didn't know how to respond. He worried he was tiring her, but she forged ahead.

"We got married. Barry and I had divorced after he found out about Sterling. He couldn't take it, and I didn't blame him. In the end, he wanted an uptown life, and he deserved someone to share it fully. I needed to be down on Varick Street. So he went off with Alice Pennoyer and they were happy as could be, at least I think so. And I did adore Stephen.

"But he ran dry. He ran out of gas. He blamed me, you know, said I sucked it all out of him, that there was nothing left after I was through with him. Which was ridiculous. Everyone knows erotic energy is self-replenishing. Of course that was before Thomas."

"Thomas?"

"Our son, Thomas Handyside Roentgen," Ida said matter-of-factly. "Born January 13, 1951, after twenty-eight hours of labor. He died three days later."

Paul sat up ramrod straight. "I didn't know you had a child," he said, as calmly as he could.

"It was our secret. We weren't married; Stephen was

supposedly with Esther Podgorny. And then our little boy died. He died. I still dream about him. Holding him for those few precious hours. He'd be fifty-nine years old today."

Ida was silent, enveloped in memory; but it was Paul whose eyes were wet. "I am so very sorry" was all he could think to say. How could this all-important fact of Ida's life have eluded him? What else had he missed or misunderstood about this woman he thought he knew inside out? Suddenly, certain lines and images he realized he'd never really absorbed—*vacant rooms*, and yes, *graveyards*, *cypresses*, *shrouds*—clicked into place:

> *the snow-blown morning when I held*
> *your tiny purple hand*

How could he not have seen it?

But Ida was continuing.

"We got married afterward, and moved to London. We wanted to have another baby. But I couldn't, the doctors said. I think each of us secretly blamed the other. But I'll always love Stephen. Always."

A phone rang somewhere in the apartment. Adriana came to the doorway, but Ida shook her head and the woman disappeared.

"And then suddenly Arnold appeared. I met him the first time in the late fifties, at Louis MacNeice's. You know the rest, I'm sure. He was still breathing fire and brimstone in those days, putting everyone on the defensive politically and morally, insufferable, really, though no one was paying much attention by then. A dyed-in-the-wool doctrinaire Marxist-Leninist, which was a damn daring thing to be at the height of the Cold War. And I was attracted to that—to his sense of injury, his conviction that the world needed putting to rights, and that it was up to us, to *us*, not somebody else, to do it. 'Make it new' was about something more than aesthetics for Arnold. Not that he wasn't the most wonderful poet."

"No one in the older generation had been more urgent, more persuasive, more prescient. And I knew he understood me, and my work, through and through. Because I'm a woman, everyone always assumes that love is my subject. And it *is* my subject. But there's a lot more going on, always. And Arnold didn't consign me to the second-class compartment. He didn't need to condescend. And I fell. Fell deeply.

"He was living with Anya Borodina, the dancer. At least I think he was. Arnold was never good with details. When we were together later on, I had to take care of *everything*, from seeing that his socks got darned to the electric bill to what we ate—and drank. He was unreconstructed in that sense. But in his mind we were equals, in a way I've never felt with anyone else. Arnold understood me as I am. And in some ways that was the most radical thing about him. No other man I've known has been capable of it. We saw each other constantly, till he suddenly up and left."

"Left London? For where? What happened?"

"I never knew. He was just—gone. I was devastated, naturally, but we'd never made each other promises—and we didn't later on, either." Ida paused. "That's how it ought to be between two people, don't you think? What is certain in this life? And if it were—would we want it?"

"What about Trey Turnbull?" Paul asked.

"What about him. He was an old friend of Stephen's. You should have seen them all at the White Horse in the West Village, carousing night after night. Trey was an utterly selfish, unreliable, overgrown adolescent—and one of the most gorgeous, most intoxicating characters I've ever known. I ran into him again at a club in Paris one night—he'd been living there for more than a decade then. I thought, 'Why not?' Yes, he was ten years younger—big deal. Such a beautiful man! And what a musician. We were all swept up in the possibilities then, Paul. You can hear it in Trey's music, I think, in the silences between his solos. Such exquisite . . . emptiness."

Ida smiled faintly, quoting the title of what was one of her lesser-known but, to Paul, most-achieved works. He nodded, and was pleased to see she was aware he'd caught her reference—though he understood it now in an entirely new and tragic way.

His head was spinning. He asked to be excused and was directed down a narrow hallway. He paused to look at the genre and carnival scenes on the walls—the wittiest and most evocative he'd ever seen.

As he dried his hands he looked at his misshapen reflection in the smoky old mirror. What did any of this have to do with him? When he came back to the salon, though, so inviting in its calm and comfort, it was clear Ida was eager to continue.

"Where were we? Yes, Trey. Soon enough it became evident that we were cut out to be friends and nothing more. He had a lot of other . . . interests. And I was spending lots of time in New York then, with Allen and Frank and Jimmy—and Abe Burack. And Bill de Kooning, one July in Springs, too. Trey detested the U.S.—he'd been living in self-imposed exile for more than a decade, as lots of black artists did in those days.

"And I couldn't stand Nixon. Couldn't bear his surly scowl. Not to mention the fact that what we were doing in Vietnam made me literally ill. I ran into Arnold again, here, at Celine Mannheim's—and, well, I never went back. Oh, I'd go for readings, and to see Sterling and Maxine every couple of years. But my life became Arnold. Here in Venice. For twenty years."

"And you truly didn't talk about your work?"

"Never—while we were writing. There were all the usual obligations and annoyances, as with anyone—and, as I said before, so many doctors. Italian medicine, Paul—you have no idea. Though some of them are truly wonderful. But they're philosophers, you know, not scientists.

"But then when the books arrived from Impetus, we'd sit down and read them together, as if they were by somebody else. And we'd talk for hours—about what spoke to us in what we'd read, what bothered and disappointed us, what we'd stolen from each other. What we'd been after in our work, what we'd intended, even what we'd failed at. What we were jealous of, too, and not just on the page. Arnold always knew *precisely* what I was up to. He'd zero in on the grief I wanted to paper over. And my infidelities, even when they were only of the head and heart, as they tended to be—until the last years, at least. And he'd rant and rave and rave and rant, and then it would be over. It had gone back into the poetry, where it belonged.

"Which is why I don't know about the notebooks, Paul. I wouldn't have. I find it extremely odd that he wrote them in code. Communicating was what Arnold cared about more than anything. But, as I said, Arnold in his last years was . . . much less available, to me as much as anyone. We grew apart, I guess I need to say, though it hurts to admit it. I think the weight of his loneliness, which is the same thing as his lack of an audience, was heartbreaking for him. He felt abandoned, because he had been. He was depressed—no, angry. He walked on the Zattere, took the vaporetto to San Michele, and wandered around among the graves, I'm told by friends who saw him there. And he wrote. Wrote for hours. But what he was writing I never knew."

Ida held Paul's look for a moment. "I guess it was these, these notebooks." She shifted in her seat. "And you say they're diaries?"

"Here. They're like this."

Paul opened his briefcase and took out a few pages of his transcription, along with a Xerox copy of the original page in code:

12 JULY 1985

8:29 caffè, cornetto
10:40 mercato
1:30 colazione a casa
15:30 Giannotti
20:30 Olga

13 JULY 1985

8:18 caffè latte, cornetto
9:30 RAI 4
1:15 colazione
16:30 Moro
20:15 Celine

And farther down:

breeze grass towel drain disappear cold old

Ida looked them over for several minutes. Then suddenly she dropped her head and bit her lip, seemingly on the verge of tears.

"I know. It's very sad. I'm—"

"No! You don't understand." Ida was incensed. "He was *spying* on me. These aren't Arnold's appointments. He never went anywhere. They're *mine*." Ida squared her shoulders and stared at Paul. "Mine."

"I see." What else could he say?

Ida laughed, bitterly now. "I don't think you do. By the end of his life, Arnold had become pathologically jealous of me. Mainly, I think, because I was still working—though I spent so much of my time taking care of him. Maybe that was part of it, too. I became unbearable to him. I don't think he could stand the sight of me."

This was another Ida altogether, very far from Paul's fantasies.

"Eventually, yes, Leonello and I started seeing each other. But that was long after Arnold and I had stopped communicating, stopped sharing our lives. He was lost to me. And what was I supposed to do, I ask you? Stay locked up in that wretched apartment with someone who despised me?

"I hadn't known he'd known, though. That's what hurts. I wanted to protect him. But people see more than you think they do—even when they don't seem to see anything at all."

Ida wept. The room seemed to have closed in on them as dusk came on, till there was just the pool of light cast by the lamp next to her. Eventually, she started coughing and wouldn't stop. Tears ran down her cheeks. She was gasping for breath.

Paul started to rise to go find Adriana, but Ida motioned to him to stay put.

At last, she was still. Out of desperation he tentatively asked, "What about these lists of words? What do you think they are?"

Ida picked up the pages again and lifted them to her face, scanning them intently and then riffling through them, stopping now and then to examine a few lines more carefully before tossing them onto the table.

"Who knows?" she said, with a tinge of resentment. "It was a long time ago, you know. Maybe they're ideas for poems, things he wanted to look up, things he wanted to remember, or couldn't forget. What was left of his unquenchable need to write. Like poor old Bill de Kooning, still painting those loopy dead canvases, as if the gesture itself, the mechanical act, was what mattered. Maybe Arnold, too, was a poet to the end, even if he couldn't write poetry anymore."

Ida was quiet for a long time, sipping her cold tea, seemingly looking at the wall. The fire in the small fireplace near the door was embers now.

Suddenly, she roused herself and turned to Paul, putting on a face like a stage actress. The room seemed to brighten artificially.

"How is Sterling? I haven't seen him for years now. How is his life with Bree?"

"They seem very happy together," Paul answered, as if he knew.

"Bree has been in Sterling's life since he was a young man. She worked for him at Impetus for years. She's remarkably astute, and beautiful, and there's no doubt Sterling is the love of her life. But after Jeannette, Aunt Lobelia produced

Maxine, and that was that. Maxine. One of the world's perfect creatures.

"That halo of dark curls, that reluctant smile. She and Sterling were never simpatico. She wasn't enough of a . . . siren for him, I guess. She was too giving, too selfless. Always there, always faithful and available. Not a good strategy with a man like that, I can assure you."

"I've never heard a bad thing about her," Paul allowed.

"That's because she was one of God's children. An old soul. Beautiful in a way Sterling is constitutionally incapable of appreciating. I'm afraid my dear cousin took terrible advantage of her—without intending to, of course. And then she died. Dear, dear Maxine! I miss her terribly. Getting old is not for the faint of heart, Paul. It's not just the physical indignities, though they're terrible. It's that the ones who truly understand you *desert* you. The ingrates!" Ida laughed incredulously. "After all the time and need and adoration you've poured into them! *That's* what's unbearable."

Ida was looking into Paul's eyes again, her chin quivering slightly, as if searching in him for something he was certain he didn't have. Though she was frail, her posture remained impressively strong. He held her gaze as openly as he could, knowing that he was looking, probably for the only time in his life, into a face out of history.

"Well, I've certainly talked your ear off, haven't I?" Ida

laughed again, mirthlessly this time. "I guess it comes from not having anyone to share any of it with, anyone who could possibly understand. It makes one positively garrulous, loneliness."

"It has been unforgettable," Paul answered simply.

"Nonsense."

Ida looked across the room through the gallery and out toward a group of winking lights moving slowly on the canal. Just as Paul was about to rise, she put her hand on his arm.

"There's something else," she said, addressing him with utter seriousness. "Something I've decided I want you to see. I think you can help me with it." Ida paused. "It's a very large problem for me, but you've shown such good judgment I'm convinced you'll know what to do. No one has seen it. It will require all your wisdom, but I'm convinced you'll be equal to it. Don't ask questions; let's just agree I'm going to trust you."

Judgment? He'd hardly said anything all afternoon. But he answered, "Anything. I hope you know how much you and your work have meant to me—to all of us."

"Never mind." She patted his hand. "It will be delivered to your hotel tomorrow."

"It?" he asked.

"*Pazienza,*" she answered. "No more questions today."

It was totally dark now. As if on cue, the lady in gray, Adriana, appeared in the doorway. He rose.

"I don't know how to thank you for this afternoon, Ms. Perkins . . . Ida."

"Thank you *very* much for coming, Paul Dukach," she answered, leading him to the vestibule. "And remember what I said."

Remember? Every word she'd uttered was engraved in his consciousness—though he had no idea what in particular she was referring to.

She led him to the elevator, then took both his hands and kissed him lightly on the forehead—was she flirting, performing, or offering him a kind of benediction? Then she smiled again, unreadably, turning away as the narrow door closed.

X

Mnemosyne

The package was delivered to Paul's hotel at eleven the next morning. It contained a sheaf of eighty-eight numbered pages of rough, ridged European-style onionskin held together by a blue metal clamp, on which a group of poems had been typed. The keys of the old typewriter were so dirty that the *e*'s, *a*'s, and *o*'s were entirely black, but there were no corrections or erasures. In their own way, they were pristine.

Clipped to the cover was a memorandum neatly typed on heavy stationery engraved with the Moro di Schiuma crest:

Dorsoduro 434
Venezia
Tel: (041)5253975

12 ottobre 2010

To Whom It May Concern:

I am entrusting the manuscript of my final book, Mnemosyne, *to Mr. Paul Dukach of New York City, to whom*

I hereby convey its copyright. This letter will direct him to arrange for its publication as he sees fit upon my death.

I further direct that all earnings from the sale of Mnemosyne *be divided equally, like the rest of my literary and personal property, between the Children's Aid Society and the library of Bryn Mawr College.*

It was signed in a shaky but readily identifiable hand:

Ida Perkins

The letter bore the seal of a Venetian notary.

Paul sat at the small, uncomfortable desk in his room, with the only letter of Ida Perkins's he had ever seen. The clicking of the radiator and the intermittent groan of the Giudecca foghorn were the only sounds.

He began to read.

MNEMOSYNE

Ida Perkins

Venice, 2010

M in memoriam

Ille mi par esse deo videtur.

Paul recognized the Latin epigraph as the first verse of Catullus's imitation of Sappho's most celebrated lyric, in which he (she, in the Greek original) likens the man sitting beside his (her) beloved to a god.

The manuscript was divided into two sections. He turned the page and read the first poem of the first part.

MNEMOSYNE REMEMBERS

Mnemosyne remembers. It's her job.
The stationary heat,
the glare, the trance,
the listless
lob; then evening coming on:
coolth, cardigan
on ramrod shoulders,
sharp myopic stare
across the meadow
where the great man's sheep
browse as in an underwater dream.

No stars: the tipsy
stumble down the hill
in utter darkness
then the age-old dance
hand held and no stitch dropped
but one word said.
Mnemosyne was there;
the only thing she does
is this: recall.
It's what she does.
It's who she is.
That's all.

Paul read on. The poems, recognizably Ida's in style, were piercing in their simplicity. This was Ida at her most purely lyrical, he thought, yet sharper and clearer than ever before—and sadder, more elegiac. The poems were stripped down to essential statements in a way that harked back to her early classically inspired work, though these—knowing, rueful, ironic, resigned—were patently not a young person's poems. And Paul quickly saw that they comprised a narrative.

The Titaness Mnemosyne, goddess of memory and mother of the Muses, was speaking the poems, remembering. And it soon became clear that what she was remembering was a love affair. But this time, instead of being the longed-for object, the pursued, the responder or rejecter, as was inevitably the case with Ida, her persona here, Mnemosyne, was the initiator, the pursuer, the supplicant—struggling, often without hope, it seemed, for recognition and acceptance, desperate to be taken in by an elusive, reluctant, fugitive, disappointing other.

Muse

I WAITED

in the sunlight
by the water
waited in the breeze
to hear the rustle
in the parted

grass to see the towel
fall on the chair
the body sink
beside me and unfold
the silver voice
remind me I was there

I might have dozed
but I don't think I did
I was so dazed
with waiting
I got lost
in time without you
time I have no way
of clawing back
stale time
that swivels counterclockwise
down the drain

time that crystallizes pain
time that isn't
life or air
foul time that doesn't
move but disappears

I waited
in the sun all afternoon
I waited
on the dock
till it was cold

And when I raised my head up
I was old

There were none of Ida's familiar erotic counterparts here, no "burly assassins," no importunate, gorgeous swains-in-waiting begging to be sidelined or shown who held the cards. In these new poems, it is Mnemosyne who pines, who struggles to be seen and answered, and often fails. At times, she seems to be fighting for her life:

I never understood
that insufferable
balderdash about
hopelessness
till now but oh now
I do now I know now
how cruel your cool
and simple
kindness is

Then, to his shock, Paul saw something else.

THE RAGE

your local raccoon
didn't know what to
make of us vamping
disturbing the peace
disturbing his habitat
new in the dawn

flashing his tail
by the dam he was
hoping to scare us
but nothing
could scare us

nothing giardia
thunder or hapless
invaders could
trample our idyll

we were alive
that June morning
only we two
the raccoon
coyote and catamount
mockingbirds dragonflies

```
bees didn't
know what to do

weren't we the naiads
then darling
weren't we the rage
```

Mnemosyne's loved one, the secret sharer of these moments of joy, and also the cause of her uncertainty and pain, was a woman.

Next it dawned on him that he recognized the setting of this exalting and tormented relationship:

```
wade the old
roadway
through
loosestrife
and goldenrod
where the
primordial
icebox
keeps humming
all night

in the primordial
woods with the
```

```
owl as our witness
while the
inexorable
hand keeps on
winding
its stopwatch
killing our time
invading our dark
with its flashlight
```

The sheep in the meadow, the woods road, the unused cabin by the wind-raked pond: Paul could see every detail in his mind's eye. He had walked there, basked in the breeze by the water, lain on the dock and watched the clouds pass overhead. Time and again he had strolled past the abandoned cabin by the turn where the woods road rose as it reached the pond. Reading the poems, he was back in Hiram's Corners on Sterling's farm.

Mnemosyne's secret affair had taken place there.

Paul also thought he recognized certain words in the poems from A.O.'s lists in the red notebooks. He would have to compare them with the manuscripts later.

A third character emerged in this tortured romance: "The Great Man," a solar deity of sorts, evoked at times with more than a tinge of resentment.

Muse

LET HIM

be occupied
offhand Olympian
let him be god
while we dither
and waver

stay with me here
in the pool
of the evening
in our penumbra
his sun can't uncover

Or this:

THE SUN

surveys
what's his
with purple pride

his piercing rays
decide
what gives
and lives

but I know ways
to hide
inside the shade

and while he sleeps
we'll shut his eyes
and find
our peace in this
green glade

Paul recognized Mnemosyne's Great Man. He had something of Sterling's high-minded, airy self-absorption. But who was the skittish, reticent object of this no-holds-barred adoration who had to be shared with this powerful, aloof man?

Ida/Mnemosyne had written this about her:

BERENICE'S

hair hangs in heaven
only for you
I dressed it
I watched it shimmer
on water
saw it reflect
and correct
and obliterate
all of our
error

see it now
falling
miraculous
onto our pillow
glinting thread
binding
unbinding
your moonsilver
nightgown

all of it mine

There were poems about a rendezvous in a fishing shack in the Florida Keys and at the Connaught Hotel in London, poems about hidden mazes and keyholes and what men will never understand about women. There were tirades denouncing the loved one's farouche facelessness; her maddening, irresistible shyness; her enraging self-sacrifice:

```
Go ahead stack his books
type for him ski
even tennis and golf
if you want to

ply him
with orange juice
bacon and sunny-
side eggs if you must

cook but don't
clean dear
remember it's
dust unto dust
```

* * *

The first part of the book came to an abrupt end without any sort of summary or conclusion, almost as if unfinished. There was a drastic shift in the second section:

LITTLE REQUIEM

the pews are
all filled with
your children
your husband
pallbearers
friends and
relations
exemplary
citizen

and I sit with
them silent and
no one knows why
no one knows why
as I toss my one
scarlet carnation
into your grave

Mnemosyne's beloved has suddenly disappeared without warning, and can only be evoked now in memory.

In this second part of the book the poems became intentionally repetitive, desperate and at times rageful testaments to a desire that has been left unfulfilled:

```
How to go on
with this
heaviness all
this despair
being kind
being reasonable
practical
organized fair
when all that I
want is to shut
the door open
your locket and
finger your hair
```

There were antiphonal poems in italics, too, in the second part, an answering voice that Paul inferred was that of Mnemosyne's lover, filtered through memory:

not like that
no I can't no
we can never
find time
no lean back
and untether
how can we ever
be quiet and
breathe
how
can we ever
no lie
here together

The later poems of *Mnemosyne* were raw, harsh, sometimes cruel in their cold assessment of grief. This was something entirely new in Ida—the poet forced to accept loss, fallibility, mortality, brought low in ways Paul would not have predicted from her previous work:

Go your
way out into
nothingness
leave me
abandon
me widowed

go your way
leave me
defenseless
just go
your
own way

The book closed with this:

MNEMOSYNE ALONE

Mnemosyne remembers as she sits
and teases at the shoreline through the haze
what she sees
she's seen for hours
for days
for months and years
she feels the sun's late rays
fall on the dock
she sees the wary deer
approach the water
gingerly at dusk
she smells the ozone
after love the fear
She sees the holy eyes
that burn the dark
and in the summer flush
she hears the rain
battering the laurel
leaves again

Paul set the manuscript down. For a long time he sat and looked out the window, focusing on nothing.

He could see it all, though. He knew who Mnemosyne's ungraspable muse had been. *Someone Sterling was constitutionally incapable of appreciating.*

Maxine Wainwright had died long ago; and with Bree in the picture, Sterling had seldom done more than occasionally mention her. But Morgan had known her. Paul wandered aimlessly along the Giudecca until it was late enough to call her. He reached her at Pages, as she was opening up for the day.

"Morgan, I'm in Venice, in the midst of an earth-shattering discovery. You'll hear the whole story as soon as I'm back. What I need now is for you to tell me everything you can about Maxine."

"Maxine Wainwright? Why? Was Sterling unfaithful to her?"

"No doubt. But this is about her, not him. What was she like?"

"Well . . . she came from an old Main Line family on her mother's side. Mama apparently caused a little bit of a stir by marrying Maximilian Schwalbe, a penniless Austrian émigré; but he made everything all right by founding Mac Labs, which went on to become one of the biggest pharmaceutical companies in the world. Maxine went to Bryn Mawr, like her mother, though she was a decade or so younger than your Ida Perkins, I think. I'm rather surprised you don't know all this, Paul. I'm sure we talked about it long ago."

For once Paul didn't rise to Morgan's bait. She continued:

"She was dark, petite, quite shy, but with tremendous warmth. Utterly without airs. She had an uncanny ability to make immediate connections with people; she certainly did with me, when we met at the booksellers' convention in Chicago when I was just starting Pages. God knows why she was there—though she was a tireless cheerleader for all of Sterling's enterprises. We started chatting at the Impetus booth and by the time I left I felt I'd made a friend. Athletic, too, a terrific golfer. I know she and Sterling enjoyed cross-country skiing together up in Hiram's Corners. And Maxine was the ultimate good citizen. School board, League of Women Voters, what have you. A card-carrying Democrat. They had one son, Sterling the Third, who works for Mac Labs out West now, I believe. I remember her saying she hadn't wanted to live in Aunt Lobelia's house after she died because she didn't want her boy growing up in the biggest place in town. Then she passed away herself more than twenty years ago, of pancreatic cancer.

"But what's this about? Why do you need me to rehearse all this?"

"I think Maxine and Ida were lovers."

There was silence on the line. Finally, Morgan said:

"I find that *very* hard to believe, Paul. Are you *sure*?"

"As sure as one can ever be about these things. I'll explain when I'm back. I learned something else, too—something tragic about Ida."

"Well, hurry home, child. You've got a whole lot of explaining to do."

Paul hung up. *Mnemosyne* was a work of genius, one of the signal works he had held in his hands as an editor. His sense of privilege in possessing this manuscript, pristine and untampered with, in being the first person in the world to read it, was exalting. He had never felt the joy inherent in his work so keenly.

But this was also an onionskin atom bomb that would blow up poor Sterling Wainwright's life. Why had Ida handed him this impossible responsibility? She'd instructed him to see to its publication on her death, but had said nothing about how. And not one word about Sterling, her lifelong editor, or nearly. Was Ida expecting Paul to deliver *Mnemosyne* to him once she was gone?

No, Ida clearly understood that *Mnemosyne* was something Sterling would never be able to accept or deal with. Was the book, the reality it represented, a dilemma she simply couldn't face, and so she'd opted to leave it to him to sort out?

When had she written these poems? The title page said 2010, but were they brand-new—or had they been composed during and after her love affair with Maxine, a kind of intermittent diary? Or had they come gushing out of her in the wake of Maxine's death but she'd been unable to come to terms with them until now, as she was contemplating her own passing? Was Ida afraid that if *Mnemosyne* was left among her papers it might fail to see the light of day, or even end up destroyed? Paul knew stranger things had happened.

How could he intuit her intentions? How well did Paul really know Ida? Not at all, clearly, despite his unending digging and delving. He'd spent all of one afternoon with her. Yes, he'd read her work inside out, or thought he had, until a few hours ago. But how could he understand what had driven her to this abrupt decision? He needed to know much more before he could do anything.

He phoned the office.

"Homer, you won't believe what's happened."

"Don't tell me you had to sleep with her," he guffawed. "She was delicious when I tasted her, but that was ages ago."

"Homer, she was wonderful. We talked for hours. And she spoke very lovingly of you. But listen. She gave me something."

"Something of Outerbridge's?"

"Something of hers. Her last book. It's tremendous. Spectacular. It's out of the ballpark, an absolute game changer."

"The truffle hound strikes again! I'm smacking my lips. Get yourself home today, baby. I want to see what you've got."

Homer hung up and Paul sat in the empty bar next to his hotel watching the light break up the surface of the oily canal outside the café doorway.

He gathered his wits, reread Ida's letter, and phoned Palazzo Moro. After many rings, a low voice answered. Paul recognized Adriana, the lady in gray.

He asked to speak to Ida. After a long silence, Adriana picked up the receiver again and said, "La Contessa Moro is not able to come to the telephone, I'm afraid. She asked me to thank you for your visit and requested that you follow the instructions in her letter."

"But I need to know more. I need further instructions from the countess."

"I'm very sorry. Donna Ida is not well. If you like, perhaps you could call again in a few days. Or write."

Paul hung up, defeated. He packed his bag, paid his bill, and took a water taxi to the airport. As he sped across the lagoon, he looked back at the campaniles sticking up over the curve of Venice's large island, and, on this unusually clear day, the Dolomites rising white in the distance like a wall of ivory. Venice, as you left it, looked like a snail shell curled in on itself. Paul invariably felt the need to escape after a week or so. Yet miraculous things happened in Venice; lives got lived, and art got made, in this seemingly moribund warren of infested calles and canals. It wasn't dead at all. Venice was a Platonic beehive buzzing with covert vitality. Its fabulous gilt-encrusted past wasn't the point; it was how the past kept gnawing away at the present, digesting and fermenting and reforming it, and extruding it into the future.

And what about Sterling? Paul pondered as he sat at the gate waiting for his flight to be called. How would he read *Mnemosyne*? How *could* he read it? He was the oblivious god in the book, who got to sit next to Ida's priceless object, arrogant and ignorant—an encumbrance, an irrelevance, the enemy even, blind, as Mnemosyne decidedly was not, to the treasure by his side. To be portrayed this way, at this stage of his life, and by a woman he himself had loved and encouraged professionally for decades, struck Paul as hard, maybe even cruel. Did Ida recognize that her elegy for Maxine was also an act of revenge against her beloved publisher, to say nothing of her long-standing consort?

No, Sterling's self-esteem could never tolerate this double-edged attack on his manhood—and from his most vaunted author, cousin, and old flame. Paul understood why

Ida needed his help in publishing *Mnemosyne* elsewhere, which had to mean at P & S. It was the only course of action that made sense. But did she expect him to wait until Sterling was gone to do it? The publicist in Paul rose up in revolt against the idea that he should postpone trumpeting the literary find of the new century to the world, even as he recognized that this was surely what delicacy required. Sterling could live another ten or fifteen, or even twenty, years; Paul would be nearly an old man himself by then. Would anyone care about Ida and Sterling and Maxine and *Mnemosyne* in 2030? Besides, who was he to override Ida's instructions?

These larger-than-life people with their precious feelings that demanded to be memorialized: Ida, Outerbridge, Pepita, Thor, Dmitry, Eric: so endlessly navel-gazing, so convinced of their significance and depth and originality. And Sterling and Homer, too. Writers! Publishers! They were all intolerable. They expected him to be as wrapped up in their stories as they themselves were. And he had been; that was the awful truth. He'd fed off their work and their vicissitudes; he'd made them the star players in a drama he'd been staging for himself since his teenage years in Hattersville. He'd lived through them and they'd floated past in their own precious bubbles, down the river past him.

In the end, though, it was Maxine, the tolerant solid citizen, the brave, good-natured, generous, "normal" one, who wouldn't have dreamed of putting pen to paper, who had been the muse of his muse's last and, he was convinced, greatest book—Ida's secret sharer, someone in and of the real world, without any of the pretension or self-concern that made this crew of narcissists so unbearable to Paul at this moment.

And what had Maxine felt about Ida? What emotions had possessed her as she consented to love and be loved by this dazzling, mercurial woman and betray her husband, no doubt for the first time—she who had so often been betrayed by him? Had Maxine been exacting some kind of revenge of her own against Sterling? It didn't feel that way to Paul. He imagined—since this was all fantasy, he might as well go all the way—that Maxine, who had always been so tolerant and contained, so restrained and self-abnegating, had been broken open by unexpected feeling, by unfamiliar passion, by a mutuality she had never shared with Sterling. Paul wanted to believe that Maxine hadn't always been the self-sacrificing victim. For once, she'd found happiness herself, and in the most unlikely of places, right under her husband's distractible nose.

As he collected his belongings and boarded his flight, Paul felt a rush of empathy for Maxine, and for her bond with Ida. Their moment in time, in Ida's telling, had a purity and a completeness he could only endorse, and envy.

And besides, who was he to judge? What he'd wanted,

as Ida had instantly grasped, he now saw, was to know his heroes as human beings—to feel his way into how they had lived, not in the pages of books, even their own books, but as men and women. He had something priceless in his briefcase—not just the last and most explosive book by Ida Perkins, but a contemporary testament to love. His ultimate loyalty had to be to what *Mnemosyne* represented. Whatever it took, he had to publish this perfect book perfectly. This at least was something he understood.

XI

Publishing Scoundrel

Homer was beside himself. He and Sally were open-mouthed as Paul recounted his discovery after staggering into the office late the next morning.

"Are you telling me Ida was balling Sterling's wife?! I didn't know the old girl had it in her."

Paul did his usual best to ignore Homer's provocations. "The thing is, the poems are electrifying. It's a profoundly moving book."

"'Moving,' my ass! This is going to turn the literary world on its tail. Get me Chowderhead!"

"Hold on, Homer. Ida is still with us," Sally cautioned. "We have to think about her."

"And we have to think about Sterling," Paul added. "It's clear he can't publish the book, but Ida didn't say anything about that. I need to talk to her, to clarify her intentions, and—"

"This is no time to phumpher around, Dukach. Purcell and Stern is going to be publishing *Animosity*, or whatever it's called. End of joke. Who needs a fourth Ace? This is a . . . a royal flush."

Homer could be a steamroller when aroused. And if he could mangle a name, he would. Paul didn't remind him that it was his decision what happened with Ida's book. He hoped he didn't need to. It was already too late in Venice; he would phone Ida tomorrow.

He called Roz, thanking her lavishly for her introduction to Ida and providing a redacted version of their conversation. He called Sterling, too. Paul passed on Ida's greetings and filled him in as to what the notebooks actually described. Sterling didn't seem all that surprised—or interested, Paul felt. He suggested they meet for drinks, but he didn't sense—maybe because he didn't want to—any urgency on the other end of the line, and they said goodbye without setting a date.

On both calls, *Mnemosyne* went unmentioned.

A day passed, and then another, in which he got lost in catching up—writing overdue flap copy, declining manuscripts, returning calls and answering e-mails. Earl Burns had delivered the big novel they'd been waiting on for the past few years, and Paul spent the weekend reading it—somewhat disappointing, but he could see there were things that could be done to make it more reader-friendly. Earl was far from the most responsive author Paul had ever worked with, but he was congenitally practical, and Paul hoped he would come to see the logic in Paul's major suggestion, which was that the wife should not die at the end of the book. Everything should go on just as before—except radically new. The novel is superb, he'd tell him; now go rewrite it.

Paul let himself get reabsorbed by his work, and before he knew it three weeks had gone by. On a Thursday afternoon—it was Ida's birthday, he suddenly realized—at about four o'clock, just as his energy was flagging, he answered a call that had been transferred from the receptionist.

"Signore Dukach?"

"Yes." The connection was poor and it was hard to hear.

The caller was weeping. "*Sono Adriana Pertuzzi, la cameriera della Contessa Moro. Mi dispiace informarla che Donna Ida è scomparsa oggi pomeriggio alle ore quindici-trenta. Mi dispiace, mi dispiace tanto.*"

Scomparsa. Disappeared. Ida, his heroine, was gone. Paul expressed his sorrow as succinctly as he could, thanked Signora Pertuzzi for calling, and hung up.

Everything was going to change now. Beyond his grief, he felt an upsurge of remorse like an attack of heartburn: he'd dragged his heels and failed to find out what precisely Ida had wanted him to do about Sterling and the sheaf of poems that were now his responsibility. Yes, he'd known she was ill, but he hadn't realized how seriously. How could he have? Had her awareness of her impending death precipitated her impulsively giving him the manuscript? Had some intimation held him back from following up with her? Would she have spoken to him in any case?

Whatever the truth, he was sitting now on the horns of an impossible dilemma.

* * *

Ida's obituary, which began above the fold on the front page of *The Daily Blade* the next morning, ran over onto two full inside pages, with photos of her with each of her four husbands, and three presidents. There was a picture of Ida with Sterling and Maxine in Hiram's Corners, and a group shot with A.O., Pound and Olga Rudge, Celine Mannheim, and her cousin Homer Stern in the garden of Palazzo del Pisellino on the Grand Canal in 1969.

Unsurprisingly, Ida's and Stephen's son, Thomas, went unmentioned in the long article. Paul noticed numerous other errors and omissions, though the general tone of the piece was appreciative, even affectionate, and, he felt, took the true measure of the loss to American culture that Ida's passing represented.

Memorial services were held in Venice and London and, soon after New Year's, at the American Academy of Arts and Letters, the colonnaded Beaux Arts palace on 155th Street in upper Manhattan that felt to Paul as if it belonged in Washington, D.C., or maybe Saint Petersburg. He watched them all file into the neoclassical auditorium with its coffered ceiling, red velvet curtains, and Renaissance-style organ, reputedly one of the best in the city: the disciples and children of the writers of the Movement whom he'd read and reread all his life. Mary de Rachewiltz, Pound's daughter, was there, ghostly and remote, with her son, Walter, whom Paul had known at NYU, as well as the sons of William Carlos Williams, bent with age, and Giovanni Di Lorenzo's curly-headed granddaughter Holly, now a budding rock singer—the whole club of the inheritors of the royalties, such as they were, if not the genius of Ida's predecessors. Her younger contemporaries were in attendance, too: Snyder, Merwin, Strand, Tate, Glück, Wright, Williams, Bidart, and Stotowski. Ida's husband, Count Leonello Moro, an elegant, short, fit man in his mid-fifties with pomaded hair, sat unnoticed in the back with Svetlana Chandos, who had come with two of her sons, as well as the Wainwright and Perkins clans by the score, in stiff dark suits and frosted hair, so different in style and demeanor from their famous renegade relation and her brothers and sisters in the art. Most of the raffish crowd in corduroy jackets and hiking boots, though, what passed for the remains of America's literary aristocracy, struck Paul as hopelessly dowdy compared with the person they were there to celebrate.

Paul remembered a luncheon Homer had given years ago at the Thespian Brotherhood, a temple to bygone theatrical greatness on Madison Square. The occasion had been the publication of a group biography of the Wintons, arguably the most distinguished artistic/intellectual family in American history, who could lay claim to having produced America's first great sculptor, her leading naturalist, and her first internationally acclaimed lyric soprano, all in one generation. The Winton descendants, though, turned out to be a raggle-taggle bunch of dipsomaniac WASPs from the back of beyond whom Paul couldn't imagine being familiar with, let alone understanding, their famous forebears' achievements. So much for genetics. Genius, it seemed, struck like lightning and moved on, leaving befuddlement and disarray in its wake. It didn't tend to deposit a residue in the following generations the way egregious beauty or physical prowess, not to mention wealth, sometimes could, but scattered its glory willy-nilly. Which was why Paul set no stock in ancestry, Homer's or Sterling's or his own. Who cared who your grandfather was, in the end? It was not where or who you came from but what you did with your own grab bag of advantages and disadvantages that made you remarkable. He'd learned early on in his work that the real writers hadn't gone to Yale or Oxford; they came from everywhere—or nowhere—and their determination to dig down, to matter, whatever the odds against them, was the only key to their succeeding. For every Ida who had been to the manner born, there were ten—no, twenty—Arnolds and Ezras and Pepitas, youngsters from the provinces determined to make their mark by dint of their own talent and hunger and grit. And Ida and Sterling had been no different. They'd been just as eager to escape their own stifling, if well-padded, backgrounds, to break away that ecstatic summer in Otter Creek, to leave behind where they'd come from and become who they aspired to be.

Nothing was more democratic than talent. And nothing was more threatening to families, be they rich or poor, or consequently more despised and feared.

Here, too, in the academy's ice-cold auditorium, while the speakers droned on, accurately enough, about Ida's Enduring Significance, Paul felt something was missing. It was all heartfelt, all true as far as it went, but the encomia failed to catch the essence of the living, breathing person he'd been privileged to share an afternoon with—and whom others here had known intimately. Ida wasn't here, in body or spirit—except when she was quoted. And then she came miraculously to life.

That was the thing. Ida *was* her work now. Her life in the world had ceased to matter, except to those who'd been touched, or wounded, by her. Her significance had transmuted into something lodged in her words. They'd grown out of the substrate of her life, just as she herself had derived from Delanos and Perkinses and Severances and Wainwrights, but they'd detached from their source and become autonomous. "*Tel qu'en lui-même enfin l'éternité le change*," Mallarmé had put it: the future was going to refine, to redefine, Ida's nature in a way mere life never could; it would anneal her to her essence, such as it greatly, or even maybe not greatly, was—though Paul was as sure of her work's enduring value as he was of anything. Time would tell. The process was already under way, and it was beyond anyone's power—hers or Sterling's or Homer's or Elliott Blossom's, or his, for that matter—to determine or even influence her fate. Along with all the other words Ida had written, the poems of *Mnemosyne* would have a life of their own. It was Paul's job to get out of the way, whatever the consequences. He had spent the weeks since Ida's death wrestling with what he should do about her book. Now, at last, he thought he saw the way forward.

When Sterling's turn came, he spoke without notes. He leaned over the podium and gazed into the packed, drafty hall, his glasses sliding disarmingly down his long nose.

"Cousin Ida was one of the lights of our house and the glories of our literature. She was named for my grandmother, like my daughter, but we shared much more, thanks in part to her loyalty to the noble and unjustly maligned Arnold Outerbridge. The freshness of her poems, the depth and strength of feeling they embody, their miraculous, sometimes shocking honesty worked wonders on the readers, and the other writers, of her time. Lionel Trilling once referred to Robert Frost as 'a terrifying poet'—a tremendous compliment. Ida by contrast was a poet who inspired reverence and love, for the brilliance but even more for the humanity of her knowledge—not only of the fundamental properties of our language and our complex and contradictory history but, most important, of our unpredictable human natures—qualities of the woman herself now fixed forever in her immortal poetry.

"All the forces that play on human beings were at work in and on Ida. This, I think, is the secret of her astounding popularity with everyone, from Brother Elliott Blossom, who is here with us in the front row, to the Common Reader out there in the wide world. Ida was the Common Writer in a way that was and is and ever shall be entirely her own. She is Walt and Emily and Herman and Tom and Wallace and Hilda and Gertrude all rolled into one. We shall never see her like again."

Blossom spoke, too, at mind-numbing length, and Pepita Erskine, to Paul's surprise, recalling her time with Ida at Esalen in the sixties. W. S. Merwin represented Ida's younger poet-peers and Abe Burack the prose writers, and Evan Halpern, now miraculously converted to unstinting approval of Paul's goddess, the critics; last of all was Alan Glanville, the rising young Stanford scholar whom Sterling had just commissioned to write Ida's biography.

Homer, never one for solemnities, left as soon as he decently could, but Paul stayed to the bitter end (the speechifying went on for an excruciating two and a half hours).

At the reception afterward in the upstairs gallery lined with anodyne paintings by the academy's artist members, he finally approached Sterling.

"Well, hello, Paul. Long time no see. How's Homer?"

"Very well. He was here, but he had to leave. Your remarks were beautiful; perfect, I thought."

"Ida and I had a very strong connection, you know. A profound bond," he drawled. Paul could tell he'd said it a thousand times on as many campuses. Paul was having a hard time picking up on what Sterling was feeling, not that it was ever all that easy to tell. He wasn't a WASP for nothing. "Thanks for your letter," he added, referring to the condolence note Paul had written him about Ida.

"I'm sorry I haven't been more in touch. Things have been insanely busy at work. As a matter of fact, though, there's something I need to talk to you about that came up in Venice. May I call you tomorrow?"

"Please do." Sterling raised his left eyebrow quizzically in a characteristic gesture of—what? "I'll be up at the farm."

Sterling was tackled by Angelica Blauner, the painter, who had been the second wife of his chum the translator and poet Oswald Fessenden. Paul chatted nonsensically for another hour with Blossom and Glanville and Sterling's daughter, Ida Bernstein, "Ida B," as he'd come to think of her. He introduced himself to Count Moro, but the man, who was out of his element in English, only nodded vaguely, clearly unaware of Paul's involvement with Ida or her book.

He also managed to stay on the other side of the room from Roz Horowitz. How was he going to explain things to Roz? She had been Ida's loyal agent for decades, one of the first to take on a poet as a client. Why had Ida left her out of the picture? *Mnemosyne* was bound to be a colossal hit. Roz was not going to take kindly to being cut out of the excitement, not to mention her 10—or was it 15?—percent.

Should he have told her right away about what had happened in Venice? Possibly. But whatever and whenever Paul told her, she was going to go ballistic, and in his bones, he knew their relationship was over. Which was a shame, because he had always enjoyed Roz, and they'd done excellent work together. After all, it was she who had sent him to see Ida in the first place.

Ida had put him in an incredible pickle. He was going to toss and turn that night, and not only because of all the cheap wine he'd knocked back at the reception. He hated being on the wrong side of people he liked or admired. Only the fact that *Mnemosyne*, sitting quietly on his desk like a smoking kryptonite nugget, now belonged to him consoled him.

And it did, he had to admit. Big-time.

XII

A Call to Hiram's Corners

"Sterling, it's Paul Dukach." He was at his desk, hunched over the phone, an encouraging mug of coffee within reach.

"Good morning, Paul," said Sterling, always the gentleman. And then, as ever, "How's Homer?"

"He's well, I'm sure—though I haven't seen him yet today. How is it up there?"

"Sunny and wickedly cold. We got three inches overnight—after I got home, luckily—and the wind is whipping it around in the meadow. But tell me about your visit with dear Ida. We haven't had a real chat since your trip."

"I know, and I'm sorry about that. We must set a date." He took a sip. "It was one of the extraordinary afternoons of my life, Sterling. We discussed the notebooks, as I told you, and a thousand other things. I learned an enormous amount. But here's the thing I need to tell you." Paul put his mug down. "She gave me something. She gave me a manuscript."

"She did *what*?"

"A book of poems. She said it was her last. And now, unfortunately, I guess it will be."

"Well, why haven't you sent it over?"

"That's what's so difficult. I don't know quite how to tell you this, but, you see—she asked me not to. She gave it to me and told me she wanted me to see to its publication after her death."

There, he'd said it.

"That's the most outrageous thing I've ever heard in my life! You can't be serious. I've done all her work, every single book, she and Arnold and Denise and Robert—every blasted one of them. They depend on me. I've always been here for them. I don't believe you. It's . . . Oh! Now I get it! Now I see. You're out to cheat me, you and that fraudulent boss of yours!"

"I could never do that, Sterling. I think you know how I feel about you. But it was something Ms. Perkins expressly asked me to do. She must have had her reasons, though she didn't tell me what they were. She wrote me a letter . . ."

"I'll bet she did. I bet you dictated it and made her sign it. You and Homer Stern. You're a traitor. A traitor! And after all I've done for you. You'll be hearing from my lawyer. I never want to see your miserable, snot-nosed little fairy face again! I—"

There was clattering on the other end of the line, the sound of footsteps, a shout. Then the line went dead.

XIII

Mr. President

Sterling Wainwright's memorial service was likewise held in the auditorium of the American Academy of Arts and Letters, a few weeks after his cousin Ida's, with more or less the same crowd in attendance. *Il Catullo americano* had, much to his pride and joy, been elected a member of the august body the previous year, in recognition of his services to literature.

Sterling's daughter, Ida Bernstein, had asked Paul, as one of her father's most faithful apostles, to be among the speakers, along with Elliott Blossom; Svetlana Chandos; Sterling's last poetic flame, Charysse Hodell; and several others. Paul, still traumatized by Sterling's death, hadn't known what to say to Ida B about his involvement in his hero's demise. He kept his remarks brief, reverent, and, he hoped, witty. Afterward, Bree, Ida, and Sterling III, the spitting image of his father as a dashing young man, whom Paul was meeting for the first time, all thanked him warmly for his words.

Homer, luckily, was not in attendance.

Before long, rumors about the existence of Ida Perkins's mysterious last book started to circulate in the blogosphere, having been anonymously planted by Homer's publicity guru, Seth Berle. The crescendo of speculation became such that Seth suggested they might want to issue some sort of statement explaining that they and not Impetus were going to be publishing Ida's last book.

Paul, though, was leery of offending the Wainwrights. Ida had been *the* Impetus author par excellence, after A.O., and Paul had still not found a way to explain to Ida and Charlie Bernstein, who, after Sterling's death, were now running his company, that P & S was going to be doing her last book. Luckily, Ida's will specified that her fourth and final husband, Leonello Moro, had no claim on her literary or personal property, as she had none on his. In fact, apart from her literary estate and her clothes and jewelry and a few pictures, Ida turned out to have owned almost nothing.

Beyond this, Paul was naturally concerned that the Wainwrights, and Ida B in particular, would be disturbed by the book's contents, which were bound to be an unwelcome surprise to say the least, and by the role he himself was playing in its publication. (He wasn't so worried by Bree; he thought she might take secret pleasure in the news that Maxine had not been an utter saint—and that Sterling had suffered an erotic comeuppance of his own.)

Ida B was not Maxine's daughter, and though they had always been cordial and eventually much more, a certain natural distance had existed between them. But Ida, independent and clear-eyed and even caustic about Sterling as she was capable of being, was nevertheless fiercely loyal to her father's memory. There was no way around it; *Mnemosyne* was going to be hugely problematic for her.

It was Morgan, of course, who came up with the solution.

"Tell Ida B that Sterling told you he named her after Ida—Perkins, that is, not Wainwright. I think it's true, by the way. Sure, he had the cover of his grandmother's name to make it all look hunky-dory, but he was always entranced with Ida P, there's no doubt about it. If Ida B can understand that, if she can be made to feel an affinity with her namesake, I think she'll come around."

Paul decided to risk it. What did he have to lose, after all? There was nothing else in his arsenal.

To his amazement and relief, it worked like a charm. Paul met Ida and Charlie Bernstein for dinner at a hole-in-the-wall in the Village one evening and told them the whole story of his visit to Ida P in Venice, handing them a copy of the manuscript of *Mnemosyne* as they said good night. He spent a few anxious days waiting for their response, but, as Morgan predicted, their worldly good natures and common sense saved the day. Ida B was moved by the book, and flattered, too, Paul could tell—the affiliation with his father's old flame made her feel more connected to Sterling, who hadn't paid his children all that much attention, not even his unswervingly faithful if occasionally gimlet-eyed daughter. Morgan was right: once Ida B had gotten used to the idea, this new bombshell of a book allowed her to identify with Ida P—and, who knows, perhaps also with Maxine, who had been neglected by Sterling in a different way.

Paul meanwhile had reread his transcription of A.O.'s notebooks in the light of *Mnemosyne* and confirmed the suspicion he'd had when he'd first read the manuscript that the strings of words distributed here and there among the diary entries had been drawn, many of them at least, from poems in the book. The diaries went from 1983 to 1988. The way the word lists were interspersed among them suggested that the poems of Ida's they'd been drawn from belonged to the same period, and had likely been written as Ida's love for Maxine was lived. This had been no brief affair, but an ongoing romance that had ended only with her death.

Which meant that Arnold had been spying on Ida in more ways and for more reasons than one. He'd been jealous of far more than the fact that Ida was still writing; it was what she was writing, too: these passionate, importunate, despairing poems to another woman. Had Ida understood this when she'd examined Paul's transcriptions that all-important afternoon? What was it she'd said? *People see more than you think they do—even when they don't seem to see anything at all.* Had she perceived then that Arnold had known all along about her love for Maxine? Had she had to come to terms then with what she hadn't acknowledged, or hadn't wanted to, before: her own role in Arnold's despair?

It had all been more than Ida had been able to face, Paul decided. And so, perhaps impulsively, she'd off-loaded the responsibility onto him.

He determined to keep these insights to himself. It would all come out in the wash, if Alan Glanville did his homework.

Paul was feeling like an ace detective, as well as a psychiatrist, as he so often did at work (at times it seemed as if Earl Burns couldn't tie his shoes without calling him for advice). And, for once, he felt he'd solved his patients' problems. He'd had a series of Herculean tasks: to fulfill his obligation to Ida and her work; to give Homer what he'd always wanted, his chance to be her publisher; and to make the Bernsteins comfortable with this untoward turn of events, all at once. And, with an assist from Morgan, he'd done it. Talk about a royal flush! If he could pull this off, he told himself, he could do anything.

He phoned Jasper and asked him to meet at the Crab the next night. They had another of their long, torturous talks, at the end of which Paul managed, definitively, to say good-bye.

* * *

On a hot August afternoon a few months later, Paul found himself on the Wainwright dock in Hiram's Corners with Ida and Charlie Bernstein, watching the O'Sullivans act up next door and reminiscing about Sterling (Bree was on Block Island, visiting her sister). Paul had brought along a proof copy of *Mnemosyne*, Caroline Koblenz's sober gray cover with its cadmium white lettering so strikingly at odds with its fiery contents. It was not lost on any of them that many of the poems in the book described the very place where they were sitting.

"Shall we stroll down to the cabin and see if we can find any evidence?" Charlie asked. A pencil-thin Nobel laureate in particle physics who held a chair at Rockefeller University and sported a scraggly salt-and-pepper beard, he had always struck Paul as complaisantly indulgent of the eccentric fauna in his wife's family. Charlie seemed to find the saga of his in-laws' amorous entanglements more amusing than anything else.

"Dad always thought a lot of you, Paul," said Ida, with just the faintest sardonic undertone. "It must be hard to have to do something he would have disapproved of."

"So hard. I feel guilty of sins I hadn't even known I'd committed," Paul answered, wondering, not for the first time, what Ida suspected about his final talk with Sterling.

"Well, he brought it on himself, in a way. He was never fair to Maxine, though he was totally dependent on her. I find it hard to believe she would have stepped out on him, though. Do you think Ida could have made it all up?"

"Not a chance," Charlie interjected. "The poems are too real," he added. "There's no fantasy in those memories." Paul was impressed that Charlie had read the book so closely.

The breeze picked up and little ridges appeared on the surface of the water. "Someone told me Ida used to say she could get anyone she wanted into bed," Paul remarked, shifting in his chaise. "I hadn't understood that applied to women as well as men."

"Well, luckily, there's no one left who can be hurt," Ida said. She raised her eyebrows in silent commentary as Charlie, who'd been leafing through the book, exclaimed, "Listen to this!"

ACROSS THE POND

Something falling
at the boathouse
someone diving
in the glimmer

I can see him
I can see her

as the sun sets
in the water

then I lose her
as I lose him
incandescent
summer shimmer.

As Charlie read, a figure appeared on the Binnses' dock on the opposite side of the little lake. The blue afternoon had moved unnoticed to rose, mottled by alternating stripes of black and gold. Then, in a perfect moment of life imitating art, whoever it was on the raft, man or woman it was impossible to tell, dove and disappeared into the silver-red water.

* * *

Mnemosyne was published on November 4, 2011, Ida's eighty-sixth birthday and the first anniversary of her death. It seems needless to rehearse here one of the most fabled moments in modern literary history. Suffice it to say that the book was reviewed on the front page of every newspaper in the country—not in the book pages; this was news! *Mnemosyne* won both the National Book Award, given posthumously for the first time, and the Pulitzer Prize (Ida's fifth and third awards, respectively). By the end of 2012, P & S had sold more than 750,000 copies, a record for a work of poetry. Just before Christmas, President Obama invited the Bernsteins and Wainwrights, the Sterns, Paul, and various members of the arts establishment to a reading of the book in the East Room of the White House, performed by America's favorite poetry lover, Oprah Winfrey.

One person who declined the invitation was Roz Horowitz. Before Seth put out the announcement that P & S was going to publish *Mnemosyne*, Paul had written her a letter recounting his visit to Ida and its aftermath, and enclosing a copy of the manuscript with Ida's memorandum attached. When he'd placed a follow-up call, Roz had refused to come to the phone. As Paul had known she would, Roz blamed him for Ida's directive, and took to vilifying him as an ingrate and a thief at every opportunity, in spite of the fact that he made sure P & S paid her commission on every copy, as if it had been specified in Ida's letter. The lawsuit Roz threatened failed to materialize, and she regularly cashed her substantial checks; nevertheless, she cut him dead whenever they ran into each other, which was uncomfortably often, though Paul stopped eating at Bruno's, where they'd had their fateful lunch.

Mnemosyne gradually became part of the curriculum in many high school and college English classes, and Americans learned how to pronounce its beguiling title (it sounds particularly luscious when spoken with a southern drawl, *Ne-MAW′-sin-nee*, as if it were the name of a broad, ferrous river meandering through the Carolina Low Country).

The book's success had consequences for everyone it touched. It was the high-water mark of Homer Stern's career as a publisher, involving as it did the landing of the great literary trophy (so far, anyway) of the twenty-first century. Homer's victory lap through Frankfurt, where he sold rights in thirty-eight countries, and at every book award dinner worth attending, was a wonder to behold. He looked the glass of fashion in his custom-made dove-gray dinner suit and helmet of white hair, the last of the independent publishing grandees, whose celebrity sometimes outshone his authors'.

But Paul's reeling in of Homer's long-desired quarry wrought unexpected changes in their relationship. Paul found that the balance of power between them had shifted almost invisibly, and he began to chafe under Homer's paternalistic, not to say patronizing, ways, which had begun to feel as outdated as some of his old mentor's business practices. Paul became more vocal about his own convictions and stood his ground when he felt Homer was in the wrong, which was increasingly often. The publishing landscape was changing, faster and more fiercely now than ever in the digital age. If things were going to stay the same around P & S, they would have to change.

Homer put up a good fight, but, being the pragmatist he was, and with a little pressure from his twin sons, Plato and Aristotle, with whom Paul had developed a rapport over the years, he ended up agreeing to make Paul president and become the firm's chairman. Homer hated letting go, and there were some difficult days when Paul felt his mettle was being tested to the utmost. Then suddenly the storm was over, and Homer seemed to settle into a quieter routine, while Paul took over the day-to-day running of P & S.

It wasn't second nature to him. Where Homer had been able to charm the pants—literally—off the switchboard operator and the sub rights assistant, occasionally at the same time, Paul found that his more inward temperament made it hard for him to project the hail-fellow-well-met cheer that, along with his absolute power, had allowed Homer to reign unchallenged. Paul knew his hegemony would need to be shared with his long-standing colleagues, Maureen and Seth and Daisy, whom he had recently made editor in chief, and Tony De Grand, his wisecracking CFO. After all, he didn't own P & S; the Sterns and their stockholders did. Besides, he adored Homer, adored his bluster and exuberance and lust for life, and could overlook the volcanic temper that went along with them, as long as he wasn't its object too often.

Homer's days in the office were different now. Sally still took his dictation, he still told his old stories to anyone who'd listen, but he managed by walking around less, and took longer lunches, often just with Sally, at the Crab. In October, Paul traveled with them to Frankfurt and enjoyed watching Homer come alive where he was still the king who helped set the fair's brash, mendacious tone. He still pressed the flesh at their booth and at some at least of the endless round of receptions. But Frankfurt was a special kind of mirror. In it, you watched everyone around you age, fair after fair after fair; and they saw you do the same. Homer and Sally had reached the "You look marvelous!" years, which meant that, unbelievably, they were old.

In the spring of 2014, Homer was diagnosed with lung cancer, which turned out to be inoperable. He left the office early one April afternoon, never to return. Paul would call now and then to ask his advice about a negotiation or a personnel issue. Homer would sound off mildly, advising him to let the issue "supturate" until it resolved itself and hang up without saying good-bye as he always had, but Paul could tell his heart wasn't in it. Sally visited Homer in the hospital and at home, when Iphigene let her, and reported on his condition to Paul and the team at the office, but before long, Homer cut himself off from everyone else, including Paul, as if his work, which had been his life, was already behind him.

And then one morning he was literally gone. Exit Homer. Paul got a call from a reporter at *The Daily Blade*, asking for a comment. He phoned Sally at home. She hadn't heard, and she was devastated. "They didn't call me," she kept saying, to whoever would listen. Paul empathized with her disorientation and bereavement because they were his, too.

He had lost both his professional fathers now, and in each case he felt obscurely responsible. Was it what he'd secretly wanted? It wasn't too long after Paul had nudged Homer aside that he'd gotten sick, just as Sterling had keeled over when Paul had given him the news about Ida. And Ida was gone, too. The polestars of his world no longer shone in the sky. Even Pepita Erskine, their signature writer for so long, had been run over by a bus a few short months before Homer's passing.

Homer was interred in the Egyptian-style Stern family mausoleum in Queens, after a cold and correct funeral at Temple Emanu-El, the Gothic-style cathedral of New York's old German Jewish elite. At the burial, Paul watched Sally and Iphigene circle like tigers, avoiding each other. The two women had always been icily civil; Paul remembered nearly freezing to death in the crosscurrents when he'd been seated between them at a dinner after St. John Vezey's historic reading at the 92nd Street Y. Iphigene had been married to Homer for well over sixty years. She had understood the essence of Homer's business, the care and feeding of literary talent. She had been an unacknowledged, unappreciated partner in the firm, frequently recommending new writers; indeed, it had been she who'd advised Homer to take on Pepita after reading one of her early filletings of white male novelists in *The Protagonist*, and she'd entertained Homer's authors and their hangers-on in high old bluestocking style on East Eighty-third Street. But it was Sally, Paul felt, who'd understood Homer; the care and feeding of him had been Job One for her.

Paul had always especially liked Aristotle, the younger of the six-foot-four-inch Stern twins, whom he called "the Philosophers." His brother, Plato, who was thin-skinned and combative, unfortunately lacked his father's style or charisma, and after a frustrating few years running up against Homer's egotism at P & S, had gone on to a successful career as an agent for classical musicians. Ari, by contrast, was wry and, well, philosophical, and his pickerel smile and laid-back personality had protected him from taking the family mythology too seriously. He'd ignored his father's crocodile invitations to join the company and gone into the *real* family business, lumber, where he had made a literal fortune, so much so that the family wasn't going to have to sell P & S to pay the estate taxes after Iphigene's death. Neither son, in fact, showed signs of wanting to make big changes at the company. Both seemed to be counting on Paul to run it for them, at least for the time being.

Paul was no Homer—nor was he a Stern, though the boys treated him almost like one of the family. All he could do was try it his own way. He had a lot of time for his pal Jas Boatwright, scion of an Alabama toothpick fortune, who'd built a scrappy house of his own, much as Homer had done a generation ago. But Jas was the only one in their age group who'd gone it alone, and word had it he was struggling. How was P & S, even if it was five times the size of Boatwright Books and much longer established, going to hold its own in an ever more consolidated, competitive publishing environment? What were they going to do when Angus called to say that Merle Ferrari or Ted Jonas wanted big bucks for their next book, more indeed than they could plausibly earn, and that he knew he could get it elsewhere?

Paul leaned back with his feet up on Homer's desk, which was now his own, twirling a Boatwright toothpick in his mouth, and feeling somewhat less of an impostor than usual. He had convinced Ida B and Charlie to co-publish the *Complete* Ida P with P & S next year—yes, Impetus had most of her work, but *they* had *Mnemosyne*!—which was sure to be a bonanza for both houses. Not only that, but Nita Desser and Rick Nielsen would likely be delivering big new books in the next few months. Something always seemed to come along to save their asses; who would have thought it would be poetry? Poets on the best-seller list! That was the magic of Ida—and P & S. But what about next year, and the year after?

Paul lounged in his Aeron chair and gazed at the pictures

of his heroes on the console behind his desk. There was his old boss, hands on hips, in foulard and canary-yellow trousers, sporting a smile as wide as the Hudson; Ida, with her aquiline nose and unkempt hair, peering flirtatiously up at the camera; Arnold, all mustache and beetling eyebrows, scowling at the world. And Sterling was there too, now that Homer was no more, a wistful, pale young man with thin arms, his chin on his elbow, staring dejectedly into space at his desk in the Cow Cottage, the future still in front of him.

And there was Thor Foxx, in his salmon-pink suit and goatee; Pepita with her gray Afro and leather-button cardigan, corduroy skirt and knee socks, frowning; Homer's Three Aces, arms around each other, black ties askew, singing at full throttle like the Three Tenors; round-faced Elspeth Adams, outwardly serene and self-possessed, sporting elegant cabochon earrings; Ezekiel Schaffner, his Adam's apple protruding assertively from his long neck; Rick Nielsen, intensely nerdy-handsome, shouldering the weight of the world; Nita Desser; Sarita Burden; Julian Entrekin; Ted Jonas.

Paul knew what mattered to him: they did, they and their headlong urge for self-expression. Their faces centered and encouraged him; they defined his world.

He looked beyond them, down onto Union Square. You couldn't erase its history: the rallies, the riots, Gorky's studio to the east, the long, cool shadow of Warhol's factory on the north (so what if the building now housed a Petco?). The hordes of gorgeous youth that streamed by him, cell phones in their palms, when he strolled on St. Mark's Place probably weren't aware they were passing the shabby apartment where Auden had written "The Shield of Achilles" either, but it was the artists who finally gave their times and places significance. Paul felt the presence of their ghosts out in the world, just as he felt them here in his office and in his head. The air was full of them. They were everywhere and always would be.

And he knew that in this at least he was just like Sterling and Homer, no matter the differences in their backgrounds and temperaments. Their authors and their work had been the ultimate raison d'être for whatever they themselves had done. Beyond their petty self-aggrandizing, Homer and Sterling and their kind had been true to their writers' gifts. Ida wasn't the only one they'd been devoted to. Their authors were their gods, despite their high-handed behavior, egomania, and competitiveness. In the end, it had been all about them.

XIV

The Man from Medusa

"Where are you off to now, Paul?" asked his sales director, Maureen Rinaldi, seeing his overnight bag parked by his desk on a Friday morning. Momo, as he called her, had cheerfully put up with Paul's lack of organizational talent list after list, year after year. Paul would have been helpless without her, and everybody knew it—especially Momo.

"Going to see the Man, where else?" Paul answered with a grin. In the last few months, his bimonthly trips to San Francisco had become common knowledge around the office. He was in love, for what felt like almost the first time and everyone at P & S knew it.

The Man was Rufus Olney, a content editor at Medusa. The San Francisco–based e-tailer was wreaking havoc in the publishing business, underselling publishers' wares to steal business away from bookstores and achieve a virtual online monopoly in both print and e-books in the process. Lately, they'd been making feints at being publishers, too, as if to show the traditional book trade how far up their asses their heads were. Paul had come across Rufus on one of the more activist websites that had transformed his personal life post-Jasper. When he'd discovered as they chatted that Rufus (screen name Rockstar Apollo) worked for big, bad Medusa, he'd suggested they get together during the upcoming booksellers' convention in New York. They'd hit it off, though Rufus didn't have the slightest idea who Ida or Arnold or Homer or Sterling or the rest of Paul's pantheon were. Content was king at Medusa, they claimed, but Rufus's expertise ran more to genre novelists and management gurus than literary writers. Which was fine with Paul, who was looking for someone who was interested in his personal as opposed to professional attributes. Rufus, who in spite of his name had rich brown hair and a broad, still unlined forehead, seemed taken with Paul's East Coast nerdiness. Paul was susceptible to his new friend's hazel eyes and winning ways and found himself yielding, often, to his insistent salesman's charms.

At first he'd called him just that, talking to Morgan or his friends at work: the Salesman. Then, as things heated up between them, the Salesman had become the Man from Medusa, as if an ironic moniker could inoculate him from his deepening attachment. Soon enough, though, Paul's irony had died away and the Man from Medusa had morphed into the Man, pure and simple. Rufus was the Man in more ways than one, and Paul was crazy about him.

On their weekends in San Francisco, they'd spend hours in the perpetually unmade bed in Rufus's steel-and-maple loft downtown, with its stunning view of the Bay; then Paul would relax with a glass of sauvignon blanc and pretend to fiddle with a manuscript (retro, yes, but that was Paul; he'd confessed to Rufus on their third date that he hated e-readers), while Rufus, the original foodie, rustled them up a fantastic meal. Then they'd lounge around with Rufus's laptops and smartphones and tablets and other devices and Rufus would try to indoctrinate Paul in the intricacies of tech.

Paul was enchanted by the lingo of Rufus's world: big data, scalability, pivoting, crowdsourcing, virtual convergence, geo-location, but before too long he came to understand that everything his guy was talking about—platforms and delivery systems and mini-books and nanotech and page rates and and and—had very little to do with what mattered to Paul, which was the words themselves and the men and women who'd written them. Rufus could make them bigger or smaller on his pads and notebooks, he could add visual elements and music, he could reformat them six ways to Sunday and break them into bits or bites or bytes and send them into the world on all sorts of pathways, but *Moby-Dick* was still *Moby-Dick*, whatever device you screened it on, and *Mnemosyne* was *Mnemosyne*, no matter how you sliced it.

What bothered Paul was that Rufus and his pals at Medusa wanted to sell Ida's—and Thor's and Ted's and Rick's and everyone else's—work so cheaply they were practically giving it away. They couldn't have cared less that a writer had sweated blood for years to create immortal poetry, or that an editor had hovered lovingly over the manuscript of a novel to bring it into the world in the form and condition it deserved. Rufus and his cohorts were all for Open Access. It sounded wonderful, and it was—for the end user (Paul had grown up calling her "the reader"). But the creator, who in spite of everything remained a virtual divinity to Paul, mattered far less to Rufus. If he couldn't get one kind of content he'd find something else, unencumbered by restrictions, somewhere else. No, content wasn't king at all at Medusa; it was more or less fungible. This drove Paul to paroxysms of rage and despair, and he found he often had to set his feelings aside when he and Rufus were together.

When he talked to Morgan these days, the news about the business was more often than not depressing. She was an extremely canny bookseller who'd outsmarted the chains by making Pages the heart and soul of the community in and around Hattersville. She had local and visiting authors give readings weekly; she had children's hours on Saturdays; she was the den mother to a hundred book groups; she supplied books for events at Hattersville State and Embryon, the local private college. Besides, she was Morgan Dickerman, and people naturally gravitated to her the way Paul had (he wasn't self-deluding enough to believe he was her only protégé, though he liked to flatter himself that he was still Number One). So Pages was still doing all right. But some of Morgan's perhaps less talented or less energetic colleagues were not faring nearly as well. The chain store across the square had gone out of business, too, which, paradoxically, hadn't helped matters at Pages.

And Morgan herself was changing. The yellow streaks in her lustrous silver hair seemed more and more prominent when he saw her, which was every six months or so. Paul didn't like to admit it, but ageless Morgan was aging. He wondered how long she could keep it up.

"I'd like to ask your Mr. Rufus if he understands what they're up to at Medusa," she'd say to him, in a tone only partially intended to mask her indignation. "I mean, I'm sure he's a good lay and hallelujah for that. But does he know what he and his posse are doing to the Fabric of Our Culture?" Paul could almost see those capital letters in neon gold, dripping blood as they burned up the airwaves between them.

But phrases like "the Fabric of Our Culture" meant very little to Rufus. He was an intelligent, educated, well-adjusted guy with a toned body, wonderful manners, and a marvelous braising technique. But at thirty-three, he was way too young to have experienced or cared about the Paperback Revolution, the travails of returns, the rise and demise of the Borders chain, or the roller-coaster vagaries of Oprah's Book Club. Trying to get him to appreciate the arcana of the Life of the Book was like suggesting he follow *Mastering the Art of French Cooking* in the kitchen. He'd just nod, roll his eyes, and quote his über-boss, the nefarious George Boutis, who was fond of saying about those old-fashioned objects known as physical books (p-books to the initiated), "I like camels, too, but I don't ride one to work."

Over time Paul found that his disputes with Rufus about the book business had grown erotically charged. They never seemed to be able to agree on anything professionally, but they had a fantastic time fighting about it, and making up. To argue better, Paul felt he needed to be as well-versed as possible in what his antagonist was saying and thinking, so he haunted the office of the P & S Internet marketing team, and as he listened to them discussing freemiums, like-gating, webisodes, and tag clouds, Paul wondered what they'd say if they knew that the quality of his love life depended on their know-how.

Eventually, Paul met Rufus's boss, Spike Edelman, who ran Medusa's book operations. A few weeks later, he found himself having dinner with Spike, Rufus, and George Boutis himself. George, who was short, pugnacious, and curious about everything, had founded Medusa soon after graduating from Williams, where he'd shared an off-campus apartment with Rick Nielsen. George, who had more than a dollop of Master of the Universe arrogance, was formidably well-read, and Paul couldn't deny that in spite of their differences he found himself fascinated, if not charmed, by his conversational adversary.

It took him months to admit this to Morgan. When he did fess up, she screamed, "Well, I'll be a rat's ass! You two-timing bastard! Now I've seen everything." After which she laughed uproariously, all instantly forgiven.

George and Paul ended up seeing each other every so often on Paul's trips west to wrestle with Rufus. Sometimes Spike came along, but more often it was just the four of them: Paul, Rufus, George, and his sharp-tongued, hilarious wife, Martha, whose first novel, about the frustrated wife of a Silicon Valley magnate who wants to be a painter, was soon to be published by Impetus Editions, of all things. Their no-holds-barred dinner conversation was sometimes heated but always stimulating, and Paul had come to feel as time passed that, unlike Rufus, George understood his old-fashioned author-centered vision of publishing, much as it differed from George's own.

One evening in Rufus's loft, after he'd served them unforgettable linguine with sea urchin, George suddenly said, over a glass of super-smooth Nonino grappa:

"How about coming to work here at Medusa, Paul? You can spearhead our publishing program for us. We've got everything you need—including Rufus. Hell, I'll even buy P & S. We'll make it the flagship of Medusa Publishing."

Paul felt the room tilt. How was he going to tell Morgan

this? But he recovered enough to answer equably, "I'll have to think this over, George. Thank you for your expression of confidence in me."

Rufus was uncharacteristically quiet while they did the dishes after the Boutises left. Paul didn't quite know how to take this; was Rufus offended that Paul hadn't jumped at the chance to be in San Francisco with him? Had he known all along that George's proposal was in the offing?

"Well. That was quite a shock," Paul finally said.

"George is serious," Rufus replied, with more than a trace of exasperation, as he emptied the dishwasher of glassware and put in the pots and pans. "He doesn't make offers lightly, especially ones as meaningful as this."

"I have no doubt of that," Paul answered evenly. "But it's a lot to take in, you have to admit. The idea is exciting in so many ways—especially being here with you. But wouldn't it mean leaving behind everything I've spent my life working to accomplish?"

"Medusa is the future, Paul," Rufus said carefully. "It's here to stay. P & S can be part of it. And I'm here. We could have a wonderful life together."

"It's incredibly tempting, Rufus. I just need to think it over in tranquillity."

"Fine. But don't keep us waiting too long. George isn't known for his patience."

Us? And you; how patient are you? Paul wanted to ask.

Somehow his boyfriend was sounding like a member of the opposing team.

Later, as he lay in Rufus's sculpted arms listening to the dryer revolve in the pantry, Paul couldn't sleep. He felt he was on the edge of a precipice and in danger of falling so far he couldn't see the ground beneath him. And he wasn't at all sure that the slapping of the place mats and napkins as they tossed in the dryer's drum in the silent San Francisco night wasn't the sound of Homer, Sterling, Ida, Arnold, Elspeth, Pepita, Dmitry—all of them—whirling like dervishes in their horrified graves.

XV

Eastport

Medusa did acquire P & S a few years down the road, along with Owl House and Harper Schuster Norton, pawns in its life-or-death struggle with Gigabyte to monopolize the retail (and e-tail) reading market. For the time being, at least, New Directions, Impetus, Boatwright, and the rest of the smaller publishing fry managed to avoid their larger competitors' fate and remain independent.

Paul, though, was no longer with P & S. Rufus and he had broken up not long after he turned George Boutis down. So, finding himself unattached yet again in his mid-forties, and having scaled the summit of editorial achievement, by his lights anyway, with the publication of Ida's *Complete Poems*, not to mention Rick Nielsen's blockbuster, *The End of Everything*—coupled with the devastating news that the Soft-shell Crab would soon be shutting its doors—he decided after much soul-searching to take a break and try his luck as, you guessed it: a writer.

"It's the most retrograde, counterintuitive thing I can imagine doing," he told Morgan. "It's got to be right."

"Don't forget bookselling!" she remonstrated. "Remember, you can always come home and take over Pages. I'm getting way too old for this fandango."

Paul had a heart-to-heart with Plato and Aristotle and recommended that they hire his friend Lucy Morello, who had been doing wonders as Larry Friedman's number two at Howland, Wolff. As usual, they were exceptionally gracious, and he'd left with enough of a nest egg to get him through a frugal year or two or three of writing. So he rented a little gray-shingled house in Eastport, Rhode Island, from Morgan's sister in Providence, and all that long, brutal winter, the coldest in two decades, he sat at his kitchen table staring at the islands that littered the water off Pawcatuck Point, trying to work on a book about Ida, a personal reading that would try to make sense of his enduring passion for her and her work.

Occasionally, Morgan and her now husband, Ned, would drive down from Hattersville for a weekend of bundled-up walks in the punishing wind followed by bibulous dinners; more often, Paul would drive into Providence to meet Joel Hallowell, the associate professor of design at RISD he'd recently found himself attracted to, for a meal and a movie and whatever else might transpire. Joel was different from any man Paul had ever been close to—calm and self-accepting without being self-advertising, in a way that made Paul feel safe and centered. "Let's sleep on it," Joel would say whenever Paul wound himself up about his work or future, or the generally perilous state of the world. Paul had promised himself he'd take it slow with Joel, but, as he watched the unchanging gray ocean day after day and tried to concentrate on his work, he couldn't ignore how frequently his new friend cropped up in his thinking, his conversation, his dreams.

He was determined to make sense of Ida once and for all, why she'd mattered so much—to him, but not just him. He had the *Complete Poems* beside him: twelve hundred pages of immortality, with her sunlit face on the back of the jacket, lifted from Ida B's snapshot of her namesake holding hands with Maxine and Sterling on the dock at Hiram's Corners. That impassive smile, like an archaic kouré's, hid far more than it revealed. He was working to find his way behind it, to get at her essential nature.

He'd recently learned something sad about Ida's last years in Venice. Aristotle Stern had called him to report that he'd seen his now-aged relation Celine Mannheim in New York, and she'd had surprising things to say about Leonello Moro. According to Celine, the count hadn't coped well with Ida's growing infirmity and had made himself increasingly scarce, spending more and more time in Barcelona. Ida had lived out her final months a solitary prisoner in Palazzo Moro.

Paul was distressed to imagine Ida, who had been with

someone her whole life, unhappy and weak and alone. He wondered if her decision to give him *Mnemosyne* might have been motivated less by concern for protecting—or wounding—Sterling, than by her pressing need, as Paul had somehow intuited, to save her last book from a neglectful husband's indifference or even envy.

Slowly, he was beginning to comprehend how one-sided, and how two-dimensional, his love for Ida and all his writers had been. It was intrinsic to the relationship; they'd needed him to magnify them in order to be fully, uninhibitedly themselves. And he'd needed to do it, to be of use, to bask in their reflected aura. It was a way of keeping his distance, of staying out of the line of fire. With Joel, he was beginning to learn the risks of mutuality. Did that mean his love for Ida was something he had to put behind him, like his fruitless enthrallment with Jasper, which had left him safely unexposed?

Ida had surely been no saint. His afternoon with her had shown him he would have to appraise her from countless contradictory angles. Yet the more faceted and surprising she'd become for him, the more she meant. Ida had been guileless *and* willful, passionate and snobbish, generous, great-hearted, self-seeking, myopic, petty. Like so many artists, she'd pursued her own desires, ignoring the consequences for others—and herself. She'd also suffered the worst loss a human being could know and found the inner discipline to absorb and master it. And in her words, at least, she had always been cognizant of her actions:

How can I tell you
the way it was?
Wasn't it always
the same way for you?
There is nothing else.
If we knew what we knew,
every instance
would have to be true.

Ida, when she was most herself, had lived the way she wrote: at white heat, without backtracking or revision. That's what her lines kept saying: this was how it was meant to be, how it could be, if only you let it. Because life was what it was. *There is nothing else.* And it was enough. It had to be, by definition.

Had he, too, left her in the lurch? Had he deserted his mentors Homer and Sterling when he'd left P & S? The company seemed to be thriving under Lucy, according to everything he heard from Tony and Momo and Seth. Daisy and her crew were finding and acquiring wonderful books, as always, and often—not every time, but it had been ever thus—finding engaged readers for them. Maybe he'd go back, if he ever finished his own book, and join forces with

Jas, or kick-start his own latter-day Impetus or P & S with contributions from the grateful authors he'd worked with over the years.

Or maybe not.

Meanwhile, Ida was everywhere. Her work was read on the radio, quoted in songs and movies, imitated, discussed, debated. It felt as if she'd never had more readers. Both Impetus and P & S were selling p- and e-book editions of her steadily; more often than not, she was the best seller in Rufus's Perennial Poets category, one of the most happening spots on the Medusa site. (Go figure!) Prizes, university chairs, even a highway in her native Massachusetts were being named for her. Her life was the subject of the new opera by John Adams, and her profile was set to appear on a postage stamp—if anyone still used stamps. The flat in Venice that she'd shared with Arnold had become a writers' residence; Paul would be spending three months there in the spring. Thanks to Ida's influence, the memorizing and recitation of poetry had miraculously become a part of the English curriculum again in certain schools. Children were learning her by heart, the way he had all those years ago.

Ida was alive, as alive as anything. She didn't need Paul any more than she'd needed Sterling or Homer, or Arnold—or any man, or woman—to be triumphantly herself in her afterlife, even if her earthly end had been hard. Her message, her genius, had been handed on, not via biology, but through the DNA locked inside her syllables. For all its greed and heedlessness, its ignorance about its past and insouciance about its future, America had produced a universal artist in Ida Perkins—in much the same way it had made a place as serene as Eastport, with its long stonewalled fields sloping down to the water, its aged, sea-stunted trees and silver houses huddled in front of the rocks that lined the shore of the Point. Some things in life can't be improved on. He couldn't imagine how Eastport could be more beautiful, more reassuringly humane. And the same was true of Ida.

Though it seemed eternal, Paul knew Eastport had changed greatly over the years. The stateliness of its vistas, its opennesses and secrets, whispered gently but insistently of creative destruction. Like every place, Eastport was always on the way to being something else, moving so slowly it seemed to be standing still to whoever reveled momentarily in its timelessness. We're all just along for the ride. You could find it terrifying if you wanted to. But to Paul it felt healing, consoling.

Paul had changed, too—he'd lost his innocence, several times over; he'd fallen and been wounded; he'd erred and failed. He'd been guilty of cupidity, of calculation, of dissembling. He hoped he'd been forgiven by Sterling's ghost, wherever he was. If Sterling had turned out to be less than impeccably heroic, it was only because of the outsize shadow

Paul had compelled him to cast in Paul's fevered imagination. Sterling was as important to him now as he'd ever been—and Homer, too, in all his testosterone-fueled glory. Time was slowly settling them into the honored niches they would occupy in his helter-skelter imagination.

Paul stared at the line of the ocean and sensed a force gathering unlike anything he'd ever known: a wave still invisible on the horizon, coming at them. It was as if they were about to relive the legendary hurricane of 1938, when the ocean had risen up and smashed Pawcatuck Point and the entire Eastern Seaboard. The shanties at Pawcatuck had been pulverized and washed away; islands had been submerged; peninsulas had turned into islands. In many places the water had flowed in and never flowed back out.

He could almost see the new wave rising to the south, climbing higher, gray on gray; he could practically hear it, roaring in his ear till it became another kind of silence. What would it bring? Dissolution. Purification. Renewal. Everything would be swept clean, and reconstituted: virgin again. Out with the old; in with the aftermath. It was time to start over.

Paul loved this view, its primal constancy even in the worst weather. He loved the repetitive heaving of the ocean. And he would love it too after the storm, maybe more than before.

He opened Ida's *Complete Poems* and for the thousandth time read the poems of *Mnemosyne.*

GOLDENROD

Mnemosyne remembers as she sits
and stares across
the water every day
hard as she tries
she finds there's no reprise
far too much
evades her failing eyes

but always she sees hair and forehead
lips meeting lips
and skin on ageless skin
she summons its faint mineral scent
and knows what she remembers isn't sin
and though she can't have back
each gone embrace
each breath each hopeless kiss
she knows she does own this

the last time
that she watched you turn
to trace your footsteps
through the goldenrod

she remembers
that she heard you call
miss you darling
see you in the fall

Mnemosyne remembers that was all

The Poetry of Ida Perkins

A Concise Bibliography

Virgin Again (Norfolk, Conn.: New Directions, 1942).

Ember and Icicle (Norfolk, Conn.: New Directions, 1945; London: Faber & Faber, 1946).

Aloofness and Frivolity (Norfolk, Conn.: New Directions, 1947; London: Faber & Faber, 1948).

In Your Face (New York: Impetus Editions, 1950).

Bringing Up the Rear (New York: Impetus Editions, 1954; London: Faber & Faber, 1955) [translated by Renée Schorr as *Mes Derrières* (Paris: De Noël, 1956)].

Striptease (London: Faber & Faber, 1957 [includes *In Your Face*]; New York: Impetus Editions, 1958). National Book Award for Poetry, 1958; Pulitzer Prize for Poetry, 1959.

The Face-lift Wars (New York: Impetus Editions, 1963; London: Chatto & Windus, 1963).

Nights in Lausanne (Cadenabbia: Drusilla Mongiardino, 1964; incorporated into *Arte Povera*, 1982).

Exquisite Emptiness (Geneva: Éditions de L'Herne, 1965; incorporated into *Half a Heart*, 1967).

Half a Heart (New York: Impetus Editions, 1967; London:

Chatto & Windus, 1969) [translated by Elsa Morante as *Cuore dimezzato* (Genoa: Edizioni del Melograno, 1973)]. National Book Award, 1967.

Remove from the Right (New York: Impetus Editions, 1970; London: Faber & Faber, 1971) [translated by Ingeborg Bachmann as *Aus dem Rechten* (Hamburg: Festiverlag, 1974)].

Barricade (New York: Impetus Editions, 1972; London: Faber & Faber, 1973) [translated by Claude Pélieu-Washburn and Mary Beach as *Les fortifications intérieures* (Geneva: Editions de la Trémoille, 1980)].

The Brownouts (London: Faber & Faber, 1974; New York: Impetus Editions, 1975).

Translucent Traumas: Selected Poems (New York: Impetus Editions, 1975). National Book Critics Circle Award for Poetry, 1976; Pulitzer Prize, 1976.

Doggy Days (St. Louis: Ferguson, Seidel & Williams, 1979; Hamburg: Festiverlag, 1982).

Arte Povera (New York: Impetus Editions, 1982; London: Faber & Faber, 1982) [translated by Harry Mathews under the same title (Paris: Mercure de France, 1986)]. National Book Award, 1982.

Marginal Discharge (New York: Impetus Editions, 1987).

Age Before Beauty (New York: Impetus Editions, 1991; London: Faber & Faber, 1991).

The Anticlimaxes (New York: Impetus Editions, 1995; London: Faber & Faber, 1996). National Book Award, 1996.

Aria di Giudecca (New York: Impetus Editions, 2000; London: Faber & Faber, 2000) [translated by Marialuisa Spaziani under the same title (Venice: Marsilio, 2002)].

Mnemosyne (New York: Purcell & Stern, 2011; London: Faber & Faber, 2011; and 37 editions worldwide). National Book Award, 2011; Pulitzer Prize, 2012.

The Complete Poems (New York: Impetus Editions/Purcell & Stern, 2014; London: Faber & Faber, 2014).

Underwater Lightning: Uncollected Poems and Drafts, edited by Paul Dukach (New York and San Francisco: Purcell & Stern/Medusa, 2020; London: Faber & Faber/Medusa, 2020).

Prescriptions and Projections: Prose Writings, edited by Eliot Weinberger (New York: Impetus Editions, 2021).

SEE ALSO

Elliott Blossom. *Brownouts and Brilliants: The Instances of Ida Perkins* (New Haven and London: Yale University Press, 2016).

Paul Dukach. *Ida Perkins: Life and Art and Life* (New York and San Francisco: Purcell & Stern/Medusa, 2019).

Alan Glanville. *Mnemosyne Remembers: The Life of Ida Perkins* (New York: Impetus Editions, 2018).

Hebe M. Horowitz. *The Ida Era* (Berkeley: University of California Press, 2019).

Rosalind Horowitz. *My Night with Arnold Outerbridge (and Other Tales from the Good Old Days)* (New York: Boatwright Books, 2020).

Acknowledgments

The author gratefully salutes the following for help and encouragement of many sorts: Hans-Jürgen Balmes; Katherine Chen; Eric Chinski, Andrew Mandel, and my colleagues at Farrar, Straus & Giroux; Bill Clegg; Bob Gottlieb; Eliza Griswold; Margaret Halton; Michael Heyward; Leila Javitch; Jennifer Kurdyla; Laurence Laluyaux; Maureen McLane; David Miller; Darryl Pinckney; Justin Richardson; Stephen Rubin; Lorin Stein; and Roger Straus.

Special thanks to Tenoch Esparza, for everything; to my wise agent, Melanie Jackson; and, above all, to Robin Desser, for her prodigious insight, enthusiasm, and, well, impetus.